Bad Impressions

Marc and Aimee Adventures, Volume 1

Michael Ross

Published by Michael Ross, 2025.

Table of Contents

Bad Impressions

© Copyright 2025, Michael Ross.

ISBN 979-8-9934184-0-7 (E-Book)

979-8-9934184-1-4 (Paperback)

979-8-9934184-2-1 (Hard Cover)

Library of Congress Control Number (Pending)

Published by Michael Ross Media, LLC

Pittsburgh, Pennsylvania, USA

Cover and jacket design by Getcovers

Please visit www.michaelrossmedia.com[1]

---

1.   http://www.michaelrossmedia.com

Dedication

To all those too old to know better than to try something new, those who tried it anyway, and those who stood by them while they did.

AND TO ANGELICA, MY greatest creative achievement.

Prologue

They, those who are learned enough in this world to qualify as 'they,' say it should be a goal of every investigator that a murder is solved within 48 hours. I take exception to that. I don't want to get ahead of things here, but I am an investigator of sorts, and I never strove (hmm, I never have striven?) . . . I have never challenged myself to solve a murder within 48 hours. That I am not an investigator of murders may have something to do with that. I am, as I said, an investigator of sorts, and without giving too much away this early in the telling, the sort I was investigating was the sudden appearance of too many originals. Originals as in paintings that is. Impressionist paintings to be as specific as I can be, again, without giving too much away.

A colleague, another investigator of sorts, was investigating some other sorts and came across a painting at a black-market auction of art and related material. This particular painting was notable to my colleague in that our company had a particular interest in it. We work for a specialty insurer of works of art, sculptures, precious gems, and the types of doodads that the rich and famous tend to collect and insure, usually for large amounts of dollars, euros, pounds, or whatever the local stop and shop accepts for legal tender.

He recognized that painting as being part of a portfolio of a recently deceased client's estate's holdings that he had inspected and certified, deeming the collection as intact and as represented. And it was represented as mostly original pieces of work turned out by the great impressionists of the late nineteenth and early twentieth centuries.

His discovery intrigued the company's executives because there did not seem to be a corresponding removal of the piece from the client inventory. Deeper digging revealed another of our insured originals from the same collection had been placed in auction where it also had been certified as an original. And another. And still, another. These also with no change made to our client's most current list of known holdings.

I was between assignments and available, so I was tagged to spend a week or two or four in the presence of our covered works. This was easily managed in that they all were openly displayed at a country inn formerly owned by the original client, now passed on to his surviving spouse, as was all the chattel therein, including the works of art in question.

Although it wasn't too far away from my home base, I called up the establishment's website and booked into an open-ended stay. Thus, I packed my bags, donned my disguise, more a mental than physical given that I had never met any of the principals involved, (I like the thought of the intrigue a disguise foreshadows, and it goes along with my romantic side) and I set off for what would be more than I bargained for. And believe me, I know how to bargain.

What's that? Oh, the murder. Didn't I happen to say I don't want to give too much away?

CHAPTER 1~ Dark and Stormy

The darkness of the night intensified with the storm.

"OH COME ON. BE SERIOUS now. That sounds like something a cartoon dog on top of his doghouse would write." Lily was not amused, even though a storm was raging outside and flashes of lightning blazing through the mullioned lead glass windows in the old mansion.

"Yeah, really," Lou chimed in.

We were sitting in the lounge at the Hensley. I was sitting at the bar, scribbling into the type of notepad one used to call a steno pad. It was opened and face up on the bar keeping company with a bourbon and water, and they in turn keeping company with the remains of one of those oversized ice cubes fancier lounges like to use.

I'd checked into Hensley Manor ten days ago, Lily and Lou already there at least a week before that, and this had been the first time I heard Lou put two words together. If my prose brought that sort of reaction from the erstwhile tight-lipped Lou, maybe I picked the wrong cover.

As far as Lily and Lou were concerned, and everyone else at Hensley, I was an up-and-coming novelist (which explains why nobody had heard of me) and I had been working on a new mystery that centered around the great impressionists of the nineteenth century of which this stolid old guest house has many. In reality, I was investigating the sudden, unexpected appearance of impressionists' paintings at black market auctions, some that I know should be hanging on these very walls.

The lounge was a comfortable room that I've taken advantage of for lunch, dinner, and nightcaps. We were at the nightcap portion of the evening, thus my presence at the bar. For meals I would occupy one of the many tables scattered about, some four seaters, some two, and a row of high two tops occupying the wall opposite the doors giving entry to the room.

The lounge was quiet and not heavily occupied at the moment, perhaps giving credence to the thought that a dark and stormy night was indeed fit for neither man nor beast to be out or about. Lily occupied the stool beside me, Lou the one beyond her. I could not honestly say they were a couple other than there were two of them. They did not seem particularly intimate at the level couples might express in public. Yet one did not ever appear without the other and they had that telepathic communication between them that intimately coupled couples might express.

Lily was on the tall side, at least a half foot taller than the American average for women of 5 foot 4 inches. She had golden hair that did little to add color to pale blue eyes. Lou was tall also. And big. He challenged the weight capacity on the stool upon which his bulk perched and none of the challenging weight appeared to be anything but muscle. Close to an inch taller than six feet, the only hair on his head was a well-trimmed full beard. It was hard to tell with his face so covered, but there were few times I saw much expression in that face.

"Marc, are the Vances at you again to try to get you to write their story? "Amiee took my empty rocks glass, plopped into it a single oversized ice cube then splashed a shot of bourbon and a stingy amount of still water. "You pay no attention to them and keep on writing what you want to. Why they most likely would have complained that Beethoven's music sounded like it was written by some deaf guy!" Her words tumbled out of her mouth at an amazing rate yet still perfectly understandable. She would have made a great voice over artist for one of those commercials with all the side effects to some new and improved drug.

For ten evenings I had been keeping company with Amiee with a bar between us. Everything Lily was, Amiee was the opposite. She stood five feet nothing but made up for it with a curvy figure. Her hair was so black it defied nature and ended in blue tips just shy of her shoulders. She was dark-complected like one with a perpetual tan, yet she had startling blue eyes with flecks of silver. She ruled the lounge from behind the bar, everything perfectly filled and spaced, unobtrusively handling the drinkers' orders seemingly by bartender telepathy.

Like most who tend bars, Amiee seemed to know more about those sitting throughout the comfortable lounge than one might glean from taking drink orders each evening. She also was ready to speak when there was someone available to listen, more so than the rest of the employees at Hensley.

It was she who first put into my mind that Lily and Lou weren't quite the death till they part type couple they tried to appear. Amiee also revealed that the presumed uncoupled couple had spent their first week on site making what she thought they thought were discreet inquiries about the proprietress, the much too young Mrs. Hensley, recent widow of the very Mr. Hensley, the very old Mr. Hensley, for whom the inn is named.

Fortunately, because Amiee seemed to enjoy talking as much as she enjoyed reading people's personalities, and because I knew how to listen when somebody starts volunteering the very information I seek, I knew just when to shut up and listen. I didn't have to ask the questions to find out what I wanted, namely that was to know about our hostess and the suspected couple, the Vances. Now, courtesy of my new favorite barkeep, I likely know more about her (that's her the Widow Hensley, not her Amiee who I admit I'd like to know more about) and my fellow guests than my fellow guests know about her (again, the Widow) and their fellow guest (me).

An intense flash of lightning lit the dim room followed by a thunderous roar as the storm continued to rage outside. Lily and Lou decided to take that as a cue to retire to their chamber. I wished them a goodnight and turned back to my notebook, keeping up my cover, ostensibly working over my novel's first draft.

They had barely crossed the threshold into the lobby from the lounge when Amiee appeared with two glasses of my typical tipple, placed one glass in front of each of us, rested her elbows on the bar and her chin in her upturned hands. "Give," she uttered.

"Um."

"You can tell me, Marc. You're no more a mystery writer than I am a lady bartender and I can tell you, those two are no more married than I am a lady bartender, and I can tell you I'm barely a bartender and not always a lady." The words came fast and determined.

"Uh."

"Oh, please. Don't play the coy one. It works better when I play that role and I'm not playing. I know you're here for some other reason. You're too good at just listening when I talk and you always seem to have a burst of inspiration and start writing edits to your book every time I walk away and wait on somebody. I know you've been trying to write down everything I say but I can't figure out why.

"Ah."

"Gee, why do you think I kept coming over and spending so much time with you?"

"Well." I know, I was beginning to sound like your favorite monosyllabic.

"Yes? Well?"

"Okay, I'll tell you," I started to say, but she barreled ahead without waiting, guessing quite accurately that I was not an up-and-coming novelist and that my visit might have something to do with the art decorating the walls of Hensley Manor. To whit:

"You're not an up-and-coming novelist and your visit here has something to do with the art you pretend to be writing about and there are a lot of that type here. Art. Not writers."

As she spoke, her eyes twinkled. Those deep, ocean blue orbs with their surface shimmering in silver, more beguiling than any art had ever done for any wall. Her face was round and framed with her thick black hair, some spilling forward over each shoulder. Her mouth was framed with deep red lips, either the smoothest, least obvious lipstick known to man or naturally the shade most Hollywood starlets would kill for to get theirs looking like in their headshots.

"...and they are looking too, but I don't think they know as much as you do. At least not yet."

"Huh."

"Are you always this dense?"

I straightened up in my chair, willing myself to appear taller sitting down than the 5 foot 7 my driver's license claims I am in a fully upright position. (My driver's license lies.) "No, no." Finally, I got two words out! "No, no, not dense at all," and then it was my turn to barrel on ahead. "I was sort of lost in your eyes." She blinked those silver speckled beauties. "Sorry. Let's do that again. I'll concentrate."

"Uh huh. That's what you were doing before. This time concentrate on the words, not the picture." And I think she winked but I could have been wrong. I often am.

She repeated saying she knew right away I wasn't a writer because I didn't have a tweedy blazer with suede patches on the elbows and she never saw me with a pipe. My puzzled look convinced her. "Okay, I see you really are listening to me this time. So now let's get to it."

And so, we got to it.

CHAPTER 2~ A Shot Rang Out

The darkness of the night intensified with the storm.
Thunder cracked! Lightning flared! A shot rang out!

"AND LAST, WE HAVE THE Vances. Lily and Lou are not a happy couple. I'm not sure they are a couple at all." Amiee had begun to fill me in on the pertinent players here in the manse. Nothing really very interesting or insightful until she got to those two.

"They are registered as Lou and Lily Vance. Not Mr. and Mrs. Vance. Their room is a classic double-double and every couple I've ever known uses one of the doubles to hold the suitcases and packages you come back with from your day out, and the other double for sleeping and pre-sleep activities." She took a short break here and gave me a look I can't describe but I liked. "According to the chambermaid, their two beds are both slept in every night. They could be brother and sister, or they could be a married couple from a 1940s family in a Saturday afternoon matinee movie. My money is on neither of those. They don't look any more alike than we do so that rules out any family connection, and if they are some sort of weird couple, what she has in brains makes up for what he lacks in hair. I swear he's dumber than a bag of rocks. A really big bag of rocks."

She went off to freshen a couple of drinks for a more obviously coupled couple than the one we had been discussing. While she did that, I noticed the storm was abating. I couldn't recall the last crack of thunder I heard or flash of lightning I saw. The previous downpour that had been pelting the windows turned into a gentler tinkling against the glass.

I thought about all Amiee just told me about the Vance couple and what my pre-visit on-line snooping told me about them. I settling on the unhappy fact that it said nothing about them, and I didn't know enough about them pre-visit to ask for a deep dive into their, on honestly any of the other registered guests', background.

"I think she's some kind of genius." Amiee returned to face me on her usual opposite side of the bar, pulling me out of my thoughts and back into her narrative. "She was talking to Loopy Louie about the Monet hanging in the Grand Lobby. It's the only copy here. All the rest of the artwork is real. Or supposed to be real. I'm not so sure about that. I gather from some of my accidental overhearing that she isn't convinced it is either."

I looked up a little confused.

"She, Lily, isn't so sure it, the Monet in the lobby, is a copy," Amiee attempted to clarify.

I pictured the Monet hanging above the Hensley's registration desk. *Impression, soleil levant*, or *Impression, Sunrise*, said to be the namesake of Impressionism. The view is of sunrise over the port of Le Havre, but in his style, it could not be taken as a true reproduction of the harbor at sunrise or of any sunrise over any harbor. It is said that when he was asked for a name of the painting for the catalog to an 1874 Paris exhibit, he replied, "Put Impression" and so it was. It is well known that the original painting still hangs in Paris, at the Musée Marmottan Monet. If the art world is wrong and the Paris copy is a copy, my visit here may end up with me doing more than just trying to solve the mystery I was dispatched to solve.

"Now they, the universal they not Lily and Lou they, "Amiee continued, "say the lobby Monet is supposed to be a fake. I don't know that I'm not so sure about that either. To hear the way Lily went on about that Sunrise picture, you'd think she was the one here writing a book – an art book!"

The storm was gaining strength again, the lightning returned, and the wind howled. The couple at the bar shivered with the last rumble of thunder, picked themselves up and headed toward the door to the lobby and then presumably to the door to their room.

With the rain-streaked windows and shadows of the trees buffeted by the blowing winds, the view outside seemed like something Monet or one of his class might put on canvas. The lightning blazed in the windows like someone set off a phosphorous bomb, the thunder took a break from its usual roaring rumble and snapped a sharp, loud, deep crack, echoing through the halls like a gun shot. The lights flickered and Amiee's eyes brightened like a camera's flash.

"I thought it had quieted down but now this storm is getting worse. I can't remember one this bad." She worried her hands on the counter between us.

I reached over and held onto those soft hands. "It's just water and wind." I tried to sound comforting. "Just don't think about it and it will pass soon." I took a deep breath and told myself the same thing. "Tell me about the Widow Hensley."

"Oh, she's a piece of work." Amiee's eyes rolled. "One day she shows up selling those little bars of soap and mini bottles of shampoo and conditioner and she never leaves. From that first day she started working on the old man. She should have been peddling body wash she laid so much soft soap on him. She had an ulterior motive or I can't spell ulterior. You know she—"

And another loud crack echoed through the halls! Only this one *was* a gunshot.

WE BOTH TOOK IN AIR and opened our eyes as wide as they could get.

"Was that—" she asked.

"I think so—" I answered.

Together we leaped out of our chairs and ran out of the lounge, saw nothing in the grand lobby but heard a crowd gathering at the top of the stairs leading to the sleeping rooms.

The lobby opened to the outside to the left of the doors to the lounge. The reception and registration desk where the faux Monet hung, was opposite the doors to the outside. A pair of doors made up the entrance to the ballroom directly across the lounge entrance. The stairs now with a growing group of guests at its top connected the lobby with the first floor of guest rooms and it was separated from the desk by an old-fashioned cage elevator.

I bounded up those stairs, wanting to get to the top before Amiee to shield her from what we might see there.

What we saw was a murmuring, crowding, gathering of guests in as wild variety of night clothes as you could imagine. Not the silk pajamas and robes you would see outside the room where a gun had been fired in a 1940s mystery movie but a conglomeration of flannel, nylon, sweatsuits, and cotton in short, long, and 'OMG you go out in public in that' styles. This crowd also differed from the fictional counterpart in that they seemed more intent to get back to their own rooms than the movie folks who were always becoming key suspects in mysterious crimes.

I pushed my way through them to get the open door everyone had just left. I smelled it before I focused on anything inside the room. That unmistakable cordite smell that can only mean the crack we thought was a gunshot indeed was a gunshot. The sight fortunately, didn't match my assumption. Lily sat on one of the double beds, head down and hands clasped over her ears, but without any apparent visible injuries. Lou was on the other bed, covered in oil, and staring at the smallest revolver I've ever seen.

"I was cleaning it and it went off." He was capable of coherent speech. Perhaps not action, but indeed speech.

Amiee stepped up beside me and looked in.

"He was cleaning it and it went off," I told her.

"Give me that! You can't have weapons here." The voice was feminine but not Amiee's. Pushing past us was a vision that *could* have been out of one of those 1940s movies. Tall, slim about the waist and nowhere else, hair the word fiery was invented for, wearing an emerald-green silk dressing gown matching the green of her eyes. I couldn't tell what she wore underneath the gown considering it went to the floor and gathered like a shimmering green puddle. She appeared to be about 35 but I knew she was at least 15 years older and that put her still 30 years younger than her late husband. The Widow Hensley. "What fool is responsible for this?" She spoke directly to Lou.

"I was cleaning it and it went off." Lou was showing off now. Two complete sentences. Well, one complete sentence spoken twice. Still a first for him as far as I knew.

"We didn't know it wasn't allowed," Lily took over. "He has a permit. Lou, get it out please. We'll pay for any damages."

"Indeed, you will. When you check out in the morning. And see to it that, that thing is in the safe until then." The young widow spun in all her emeraldness and disappeared down the hallway which had already emptied of the onlookers. (They would never do in that 1940s movie. They would have all oooed and awed at the imposing figure and would have had to be scattered, while being reminded that this wasn't a movie.)

Amiee and I were the only two left standing there. Lily looked over to us in the doorway and motioned us into the room. We looked at each other, silently concluded that we were in no danger, and stepped inside.

The room was generous in proportions. All the Hensley rooms were of a good size, each furnished with either two double beds or a single queen. Nightstands on the outsides of these two doubles plus one between matched the dresser and desk along the wall opposite the beds which were to the left of the door located in the center of the wall separating room from hall. A large bathroom with a small vanity, large tub and separate shower, and two closets filled the space beyond the wall opposite the door.

Amiee slid into the desk chair while I leaned against the dresser. Lily closed the door and returned to her bed and sat at the foot of it.

The cordite smell was lessening and you could now make out the warm scent of a recent shower spilling from the bathroom. And something else. Something trying to imitate nature.

"He really was cleaning it, and it really did go off. Accidentally." She bit off the last word while throwing a look at Lou as fatal as anything he could have fired from the handgun in his lap. "He cleans it every night before he goes to bed. The way he massages it with that oil you'd think he was ... you know."

We knew.

Lou wiped the oil from his hands and the revolver, a Smith and Wesson 43C, a miniature eight-shot dynamo that at just a little over six inches long, fit comfortably within the palm of Lou's hand. He checked that it was fully unloaded then gently packed it into a small hard-sided case about the size of a paperback novel with its interior foam lining custom cut to the gun's dimensions.

As he clicked shut the case and twisted the key in its lock, Lou said perhaps more to himself that to us, "I don't know how that happened. My finger was never inside the trigger guard. I carry this gun everywhere I go. If I'm wearing something with a pocket, I'm carrying this gun. And I always wear something with a pocket except to the shower." Who knew Lou had the power of speech? "Something isn't right here." And that would be the last example of it that we would hear.

CHAPTER 3~ A Woman Screamed

The darkness of the night intensified with the storm.
Thunder cracked! Lightning flared! A shot rang out!
A piercing scream filled the air!

THREE OF US, LOU, AMIEE, and I, stepped down the stairs to the main floor, our steps echoing through the empty lobby. Lou turned toward the reception desk where the inn's safe would become the Smith and Wesson's home for the night. Amiee and I turned in the opposite direction to the lounge.

"Goodnight Lou!" Amiee called out, trying to be cheerful. I might have heard a grumbled reply.

"I'm really supposed to close at midnight, and we passed that a while ago. I can't go to bed like this. I'm still shaking. I mean it looks like a cap pistol but that was a real gun that went off!" She paused for just a bit, wrinkled her nose, and turned toward me. "I have better bourbon up in my room. Let's go talk a while."

I helped her put the lounge bar in lockdown mode, scooping up some dirty glasses while I heard her doing what she needed to do, capping open bottles and stretching plastic over the cut fruit in the garnish trays. She busily found a place for everything and put everything in it. She punched a few buttons on the cash register, turned a key on its front, hustled me out the door and turned another key in its front. As the bolt turned and clicked into place she said, "Let's go. I need that drink. When was the last time you heard a bartender say that?"

OUTSIDE OF THE WIDOW herself, Amiee was one of only three employees who lodged permanently at the Inn. The others were Grayson, the manager who had been there since day one, and the one-man maintenance staff who everyone just called Junior. Amiee's mini-suite was at the farthest end of the employees' wing.

"Did you notice in their room, both beds were turned down?" She wasted no time getting into a recap of what we just saw. "And that look she gave him! What do you make of that? I'm telling you they are not what they what to seem to be."

I was busy noticing Amiee's room. Here I found proof to the adage, perfection at work, disaster at home. Well...that was unfair. It was not up to frat house level (or would that be down to?), but it did a good job defining messy. The once two double-double rooms were turned into a two-room suite and the space previously housing one of the guestrooms now served as a sitting room. It held a small table and two chairs, presumably a space to eat. Along the wall where the Vance's classic double-double held a writing desk and a television stand, was a small writing table, and another table that held coffee maker, microwave, some mugs and plates, and a small wicker basket holding flatware. A television stand and a small bookcase occupied one wall. No flat surface was empty, and the backs of all the chairs held various articles of clothing from pantyhose to the black blazer she wore over her white shirt when at work. Perhaps I was too hard calling it messy. Unkempt may have been a better description. But I may hold judgement, not that I am or have any reason to be judgmental, considering there was an entire room unseen by my eyes.

As she found a couple of water glasses and set out to prove bartenders can still tend at home, Amiee went on to tell me Lily and Lou showed up a week before I did and immediately started asking about the art at the inn. She kicked off her shoes and sighed a deep sigh of relief. She crossed the room, flopped into the corner of the loveseat in the center of the long wall, and stretched her legs. Good legs, stockinged in a barely black shade of nylon, dangled over the front of the love seat. From the hem of her black skirt her legs almost reached to the floor. That black skirt with a men's cut white dress shirt and the previously noted blazer made up her work uniform.

She bounced up from her position on the love seat to the counter, moved the drink fixings to in front of where I was sitting as said. "Pour me a big one after you make another one for yourself, please," she said as she disappeared through the door to the bedroom of her suite.

From behind the partially open door she called out, "It's no secret that Mr. Hensley was one of the biggest collectors of the Impressionists. His favorite was Monet but they're harder to come by than a bourbon bottled outside of Kentucky. The collection is mostly Morisot. He loved the way she used shadow even though her work was a lot of open scenes and bright indoor settings. He said he lived his life in the shadows wherever he could find it and appreciated that someone was able to master them." A pause, and then she reappeared now clad in an old-fashioned peignoir of white satin and lace, with its matching robe hanging open around her. The white of the material positively shimmered against her dark hair and complexion.

"I think she's up to no good," she said.

"Morisot?" I interrupted my own thoughts while handing over a substantially bourbon filled glass that she took, sipped, and gave a thumbs up. I went on, "If she is up to no good it's really not good. She died like in the 1890s"

"No, silly. Lily Maybe Vance."

"Maybe Vance?"

"I don't believe Lily and Lou are Vances any more than I believe they are anybody of the same last name. They probably picked that name out of phone book." She stopped long enough to let a puzzled look settle on her face. "Do you suppose there are still phone books?"

We settled into a thoughtful yet comfortable silence. When we resumed talking, we talked for a while about phone books, the Maybe Vances, the Hensley collection, working at a small inn-type hotel, and the best ratio of bourbon to water to sustain late night conversation. After a while, we turned our talk to life in general, love in the modern world, and the pursuit of happiness. Sometime during our last round of topics, I moved to join her on the love seat. We moved closer and pursued some happiness and gave credence to whoever knew how to name furniture.

She was a wonderfully warm person, comfortably fitting into my arms like they had been sculpted for her to settle into. She sighed another deep sigh, and smiled at me with her eyes, those deep blue, silver highlighted shimmering orbs that lit up her face. Her dark, soft skin glowed. She pressed her cheek against mine, holding it there, letting me feel her wonderful warmth. She pulled her head back and looked so intently at me, I was certain she could read my mind. She could.

"Kiss me," she whispered. She closed her eyes, parted her soft, red lips, and moved back toward me. "Kiss me and please don't stop."

And stop we didn't. We stayed in that embrace until we didn't and then stopped only to move ourselves into the other embrace and from there into yet another. It was good. It was very good. It could have gone on all night long. It almost did. We stayed in each other's arms that night doing what two youngish people do when they discover each other. We stayed that way right until dawn. Right until the lady screamed.

CHAPTER 4~ A Ship Rode on the Waves

The darkness of the night intensified with the storm.
Thunder cracked! Lightning flared! A shot rang out!
A piercing scream filled the air!
Large ships filled the small harbor.

WE RAN INTO THE HALL toward the piercing wail. Grayson was already where all the hallways meet to form the second-floor lobby. He did a double take when he saw me coming from the employee residence wing but didn't lose a step as he pounded his feet against the floor hurrying to the scream's source. We pivoted through the upper lobby and ended up in front of the same door we stood at just a few hours earlier. The door was closed but we heard not a fat lady tuning up for her aria, but Lily screaming at a volume and pitch that made her sound like she was standing next to us.

"Miss Vance! Miss Vance! Open the door! It's Grayson the manager," he said as he pounded on the on the door. "Miss Vance! Can you hear me?"

"Don't you have a key?" I shouted at Grayson. "Just open the door!"

Grayson's keys jangled as he fumbled with his ring until he found the guest room master. After two unsuccessful attempts he finally slid it into the lock, turned it, and threw the door open.

Lily stood in the doorway to the bathroom, her robe loose around her body, holding a towel clutched tightly just under her chin. She continued to let out ear splitting screams, quiet only long enough for her to refill her lungs before hurling another howl into the hall. I wasn't certain she realized we were in the room. Her eyes were fixed on the bed against the far wall. There lay Lou, his unseeing eyes stared back at Lily, and what appeared to be a length of some sort of rope coiled around his neck.

Amiee pushed her way past Grayson and I, into the room, and over to Lily. She led her by the arm to the desk chairs, settling Lily into one and herself into the other. She took a position that put her between the sitting Lily and the prone Lou. The movement quieted Lily but for her heaving breaths, and she now sat staring at the floor. What had been just a handful of hours that now seemed a lifetime ago, Lily had sat in that same chair telling us how Lou cleaned his gun every night. She was sitting there again. In that same chair. In front of that same desk.

Odd. Something didn't seem the same. Something was different. Something was off. Something besides the dead guy on the bed.

Lily's keens slowly turned to sobs, then to deep, ragged breaths, finally calming almost to normal breathing. She picked up her head, looked toward Lou motionless in his bed and let loose another yowl. Amiee turned Lily's head into her shoulder and held on tighter.

"We need to get her out of here!" Amiee said over Lily's shoulder, bringing me out of my pondering.

Grayson snatched his pass key from the lock. "The room across the hall is empty. I'll open it, you two can walk her over. I'll inform Mrs. Hensley and then call the police." He disappeared down the stairs. I couldn't believe with all the screaming the Widow, and all the other guests, were not already informed that something had gone wrong this morning. Terribly wrong.

Amiee helped Lily stand up and swung her toward the door. I went over and stationed myself to make us three abreast. With Amiee on one side of Lily and me on the other, we looked like the Keystone Kops trying to get through the door. "I have her," Amiee said, and I stayed behind while they managed to cross the threshold successfully and moved across the hall.

I walked over to take a closer look at the late Mr. Vance. Being careful not to touch anything, I got close enough to get a good look at that rope.

"Mr. Crossley! Come out of there!" The Widow Hensley would show up just then. "We are supposed to lock this room until the police get here. They're sending someone right over."

"Yes! Ma'am," I straightened up and marched into the hall, then she pulled the door closed and returned to the main level, heels clacking against the polished surface of the stairs.

I wanted a better look at whatever it was around Lou's neck. I had a thought about it, and the thought was that it couldn't be, but then things that couldn't be have been and always will so who am I to say it isn't without a good look. But all I was getting now was a good look at the hallway side of the door.

The unmistakable sound of a throat being cleared brought me out of my mini-funk. Grayson, who had returned with the Widow, stayed behind. Grayson has either no first name or a first name nobody ever got out of him. Even his brass name tag just read "Grayson" etched in black above the word "Manager" on a second line. He was a proper gentleman of a certain age. His hair was steel gray, too thick and too much of it for his age, however uncertain that was. He also sported a mustache of a style last seen on William Powell during his heyday. Grayson had been at the Hensley longer than the Widow, previously serving as the master's gentleman's gentleman. Where he came from before that was as apparent as his first name. When Mr. Hensley decided to convert his country estate into a country manor for profit, Grayson became the default choice to manage the endeavor.

"The police will be here shortly," Grayson said to me. "They will want to talk to Miss Vance, you, Amiee, and I suppose anybody else on the floor who heard or saw anything." He looked up and down the hall and sighed. "All the time I have been in service in this building nothing like this has ever happened."

"Yeah, and old Lou hadn't been here for too much of that time, and I bet this is a first for him too." I don't know why but Grayson's remark irritated me. It just wasn't nice.

INSIDE THE ROOM ON the other side of the hall beyond the open door, Lily looked and sounded more normal. She was sitting in a large, overstuffed chair common to the queen bed configured rooms, and Amiee was making soothing sounds while facing her sitting at the foot of the bed. Lily was holding onto a glass of water with both hands as if it would fly away if she let go. Together they looked at me as I entered the room.

"The police will be here soon," I informed the ladies. "They're going to want to talk to all of us. Lily, are you up to it? If not, I'm sure we can get them to at least start with everyone else and give you more time to—"

"No," Lily sniffed. "I'll be okay and do what they want. The sooner they get started the sooner they find whoever did this to my Louie!" She sounded composed but looked on the verge of falling back into uncontrolled heaving breaths.

Amiee took the water glass from Lily, "Come on dear. Take some deep breaths. Slow and easy. That's the way."

Lily started breathing more normally. Realizing she was still clad only in a bathrobe, she clutched it again, pulling it more tightly around herself.

Amiee looked up and me and said, "We're going to my room. It's going to be challenge but I will find something to fit her so she doesn't have to see the police in just a bathrobe." She reached out to Lily, holding her hand as she rose from the chair. "Come on dear. Let's find you something to change into. I have a nice, flowered dress that somehow has grown too small for me. It might be a little short on you, but we will work with it."

As they started out for the employee hallway, Grayson, who I had forgotten was still behind me, stepped aside and said, "I better get to the desk and relieve Mrs. Hensley," and walked out.

I looked around the empty room and announced to no one, "I guess I'll go too."

I WALKED BACK INTO the hall and again I stared at the door across from where I stood. That door, that locked door standing between me and the late Lou Vance. I didn't know if it worked into my investigation but someone who was interested in art at a location where there seemed to be an exceptional interest in art ends up dead in obvious unnatural circumstances was too much of a coincidence not to look into. I wanted another look at that whatever it was that was playing the part of a rope wrapped around his neck.

I rocked back on my heels and I wondered.

Doing as I had been taught so many years ago, I looked both ways before crossing. Seeing no one coming I crossed the hall and rattled the knob. And discovered in her haste to hurry me out of the room, the Widow had closed the door but not locked it!

I had pushed it halfway open when I heard footsteps on the stairs and Grayson saying to somebody, "It's the first door on the right. I have the key," and then footsteps fell onto the landing. Coming closer in the hall!

I panicked! I didn't dare step backward or they would see me exiting the room. I couldn't go forward and say I had just stopped in for a morning coffee with my good friend Lou. I couldn't rush in and hide in the closet or the bathroom as they surely would open all the doors. The footsteps grew louder. That may have been in real life or my imagination but in whichever it was, they were almost here. 'I panicked!' was an understatement. I took a deep breath and let instinct take over. I stepped all the way in, closed the door, and dove under the bed, the very bed currently occupied by my good friend Lou. And him without any coffee to offer his good friend me this morning.

I heard three pair of shoes step in, wriggled myself around then saw those three pair of shoes. A voice that sounded a perfect match for the scuffed black service boots growled, "We just want a quick look around in here before the crime scene techs get in. How about if you get all the people on that list I gave you together in that bar right where we come in."

"Yes, sir. I'll do that and have them all assemble in the lounge," and Grayson's quarter brogues smartly turned toward the hall and walked out.

While the two cops, Service Boots and Nondescript Oxfords, were rummaging above me, I realized I wasn't alone under the bed. I felt around and sensed something solid. Wood. Why would there be wood? I felt around some more and could identify what felt like four pieces. Very straight, but not very bare. I felt wood, I felt staples, I felt canvas. And I felt something wet. Hmm.

I was certain the wood pieces that I felt were the remnants of a canvas stretcher. Why was it wet? Ignoring the opening and closing of doors and drawers, I reached around some more until the back of my hand touched glass. Not like broken glass. A drinking glass. Careful not to touch the glass with my fingers, I pressed those very fingers into the wet spot, brought them to my nose, and gave them a sniff. Hmm. Oh. Oh!

"Alright, let's go see what our witnesses have to say," Service Boots said to Oxfords. And that was my cue to get ready to sneak out behind them.

I WAITED UNTIL I HEARD the lock click then I shimmied out from under the death bed, unlocked then cracked open the door, and checked the hall. Nobody. Good. I ran to my room, hastily changed, then back out into the hall, and down the stairs. I slipped into the lounge just as Service Boots was cautioning everybody not to leave "these here premises." I took a seat next to Amiee. I whispered out of the side of my mouth, "I know how Lou died."

"Duh. We all do, we saw him," she side-mouth whispered back.

"But I saw the murder weapon "

"What do you mean? We all saw it. I mean I know I didn't want to look but how could you not see that he was strangled with that ropey thing?"

"That thing didn't kill him. He was already dead when it got wrapped around his neck."

"No! Who'd want to strangle a dead man?" That wasn't a whisper.

Service Boots looked over at us and said, "Well, by all means speak up. In fact, we'll start all our little chats right now and we'll start with the chatterbox in the corner. The rest of yinz can wait here." He pointed to Amiee, "You come with me to that little office behind the desk."

As Service Boots led Amiee away, I reached out and stopped Grayson. "Is there an inventory of all the art here at the inn."

"Certainly, there is," he said in his former life as a butler tone. "In every room on the desk is a copy of *The Works at Hensley Manor* depicting each piece and where it's displayed." Somehow, he managed to convey, politely of course, that I had just asked the most ridiculous question in the history of Hensley Manor, if not of all time.

I thanked him (I'm not sure why) and ran out of the lounge, sprinted up the stairs, jogged down the hall to my door, and made straight to the desk. There it was, on the desk, under my briefcase that I plopped there, opened, and left in place over a week ago. Duh! A little nudge one way or another and I could have perused it every day for the last week. Duh! Again. So now we know why I scored so high on Grayson's ridiculous question meter.

I flipped through the pages, each depicting a work of art, identifying the piece, the artist, and the display location. It seemed to be alphabetized by artist, which seemed a ridiculous way to arrange it, since I wasn't interested in the artist. Fortunately, I had an idea what and by whom what was that I was searching for, so I didn't have to go through page by page. I turned to the 'S' section and continued until my subconscious told my conscious to stop. It spoke up when I got here.

Sailing Ship on the Horizon, 1880
Henry Smith, American, 1854-1907
Guest Room 201

CHAPTER 5~ Cannons Roared

SO NOW I HAD SOMETHING to think about. Some things. And that was, or they were, where did that painting go, who would do that to an original, was it an original, and did I really not move my briefcase in over a week? I mulled over these and a couple others as I walked back downstairs to the lounge.

I caught up with Amiee. She had changed into her work clothes and was prepping the garnish trays behind the bar. The hum of a crowd chattering hung in the air. "As long as all these people are hanging out here, I'm opening up. Oh Marc honey, by the way," she looked up from slicing limes, the citrusy scent hovering above her mini-cutting board. "Sergeant Duncan is not happy with you."

"Who and why?" She slapped my wrist as I reached for an olive that rolled out of its compartment. "Hey!" I snapped. "I haven't had breakfast yet."

"I'll ask Cook to make you an eggy muffin. How does that sound?"

"Not as much fun as pinching olives but more filling."

She rolled her azure peepers like I was a toddler eating everything but anything substantial.

"Now again," I asked again, "who and why?"

"Hold on for a minute." She walked to far end of the bar and pushed open a swinging door, releasing the mouthwatering aroma of bacon cooking. "Cookie! A breakfast muffin please!" She looked back to me, "Cheese? Of course you do." Then into the doorway, "with cheese!"

"Now, one more time, who and why?" I asked again as she continued slicing limes.

"Who and ... Oh right. Detective Sgt. Duncan. He's the head honcho on the police squad roaming around here. He and his buddy, detective some kind of grade Ness, no I'm not kidding, were all hot you weren't here when they finished up with me. They have the night maid in with them now but that's going to be quick. I didn't even know she was here last night." She made a funny face like she had just taken a bite of the lemons she was now slicing. "Probably was in the linen closet with Junior. Or a bottle."

"Speaking of bottles," I jumped in, "what did Lou usually drink?"

"He didn't." Lilly moved on to stacking coasters, bar napkins, and stirrers in their respective trays and holders. "He was a health nut. If he had anything here it was plain water. He claimed he only drank natural essences. Now tell me, what's more natural than essence of corn?" She stopped and looked up at me. "Yoohoo! Are you listening?"

"I was thinking what that was."

"Essence of corn? Bourbon, duh. Remember? You mix it with a little water and sip, sip?" I suppose I still had that glazed look because she spoke up louder, "Hey! Marc! You with me? What's wrong?"

"Oh no, no. I meant I was thinking what Lou meant by natural essences."

Amiee thought a bit while she arranged her bar keepers' tools. "Well for him, probably essential oils. He was always talking about them and how he'd add something natural to his lotions and creams and probably his gun oil too now that we know he used that. I guess that's what he drank, too." She looked up at me. "Now what?"

"You can't drink essential oils. They're toxic taken internally. I wonder," and looked like I was wondering, "what he added to his oil. Did he ever say?"

"I don't remember. But I do remember that whenever he started talking about it, or if I should happen to get of whiff of it on him, I started thinking about Australia."

"Wait, what?"

"Australia. You know, down under. Home of crocodiles and kangaroos."

"And emus and koala too," I added.

She made that lemon face with her still very full very red lips. "Don't give me that look," she said with that look. "You started it."

From her side of the bar Lily rested her elbows on the bar top and rested her chin in her hands like she liked to do. "When I was in high school a hundred years ago, we went to the dedication of the Sydney Opera House. Our art teacher was a kinda sorta wannabe architect and somehow convinced the school that would be a better senior trip that going to the Paris museums. It was the first and probably only time I'd be out of the country, and I really wanted to go to Europe. When else will I ever see the Eiffel Tower, Notre Dame, the Louvre? You know, I hadn't thought about all that for a long time until Lou brought up his oils. I wonder why"

"What?"

"Why what?"

"You wonder why. Why what?"

She shook her head making her thick hair look like it was swinging in slow motion. "I wonder what it was that made me think of Australia."

"It will come to you." I shifted gears while I shifted on my bar stool. "How's Lily doing?"

Amiee's smile faded and she looked serious for the first time since I sat down. "Maybe I was wrong about her," she said. "She's really upset. She said she went into take a shower and left Lou sitting on his bed still sulking about not having his little cap pistol and harping about feeling naked and vulnerable without it. She tuned him out and went in for a long, hot shower and now regrets the long part of long and hot. I took it she wasn't happy by the whole banishment handed down by Mrs. Hensley. I figure she was unhappy because she figured they had to check out before they got to do whatever they came here to do. And get this. They really were a couple. They'd been—"

"Crossley!" A voice boomed louder than the previous night's thunder, startling me into that sit up straight position you get whenever your mother uses your full name to get your attention.

"Uh oh. It's the coppers, big guy." Amiee grinned a big cheesy smile and pointed behind me with her chin. "They found ya," she drawled in a poor imitation of what she must have thought a mob moll would sound like.

The detective formerly known as Service Boots loomed behind me. "Crossley, you're up!"

"Yessir," I mumbled and turned with him to go to reception desk. "Hold that thought," I said over my shoulder, and my favorite barmaid flashed a real smile at me.

WE EXITED THE LOUNGE into the Grand Lobby where the sound level was higher than that comfortable hum I just left in the lounge. The crime scene techs were clomping down the stairs to the second floor. I heard the metal clatter of an ambulance gurney being bustled into the seldom used ornate cage style elevator next to them.

The distinct sound of the diesel engine of the coroner's van rose and waned every time the front doors slid open.

Duncan kept his pace, and I stayed right with him, through the central lobby, into the reception area, to the registration desk, through the little side gate, behind the counter, and into a large closet that had been converted into a small office.

Sgt. Duncan walked behind the mini desk and sat in the too little for him chair while Detective Ness perched on the desk's corner. I took the one guest chair. From the corner of my eye I could see Grayson tending to someone on the other side of the counter, but not who that someone was. He accepted a small package about the size of a deck of cards and spun on those quarter brogues to access the inn's safe. He nestled the little package I assumed next to the other little package nestled there since Lou dropped it off last night, closed the door, spun the combination dial, then— BOOM!

"Geez Us!" Ness shrieked and jumped up from the desk like it was the hot part of a griddle. He fumbled his service revolver out of the holster clipped to his pants belt. "What the! Who did! Holy cannon fire! What in all that is holy was that?"

CHAPTER 6~ The Battle Was On

The darkness of the night intensified with the storm.
Thunder cracked! Lightning flared! A shot rang out!
A piercing scream filled the air!
Large ships filled the small harbor.
The cannons' roar broke the morning calm!
The sides battled on.

I NEARLY GOT RUN OVER by the two policemen in their rush to get to the lobby. I was a step behind them when we reached the smoke-filled room with alarms blaring. The crowd that had been straggling into the lounge was running for the main door, that formerly comforting hum now a loud cacophony accompanied by shoes pounding the terrazzo floor.

Amiee spotted me from the lounge doorway and beckoned me over.

"What's going on?" she asked as she grabbed me by the shoulders and shouted to my face over the din of alarms beeping and people bleating.

"I'm not sure." I shouted back and shook my head in case she still couldn't hear me. While keeping her in front of me, her back to the lounge opening, I turned my attention toward the action in that once great hall. "I think it's the elevator. That's where the smoke seems thickest."

I took a step away from the lounge, deeper into the lobby, but there was so much smoke I could have been standing on top of it, whatever it was I was looking for, or at, and not know it. Whatever that might be. Something seemed off about that smoke. It was almost too thick, and it didn't smell right. I'm not sure I know what an explosion is supposed to smell like, but this smelled like your house when the furnace kicks on the first time on a chilly autumn morning. I felt myself shaking my head again "I can't tell anything from here."

Detective Ness emerged from the smoke, barking orders into his cell phone. "...and get the county CSI truck. I don't think we're going to have the equipment for this one." He looked to us and said, "Yo, you, bar lady!"

A fire truck with its siren winding down roared onto the porte cochere. Two fire fighters hauling a first responder kit rushed through the door. Ness turned his attention to them. "Far corner. Two hurt, one pretty bad, and one dead guy from before, maybe another joined him. It's actually clearer back there. The elevator shaft is venting the smoke. No fire."

The fire fighters gave a thumbs up and clambered their way through the lobby. The front door swished open again and two more took their places. Ness continued with them. "Explosion, no fire. That's mostly dust you see here." They said something to him that I didn't get and rushed deeper inside the building. He turned back to us. "Okay, bar lady, did you..."

"Amiee," Amiee said.

"What"

"Amiee," Amiee repeated, "Amiee with an I-E-E, not a Y"

"What. why?"

"No, no why, no letter Y. It's A -M- I-E-E, no Y.

"Why Y, or no Y?"

"I don't know, maybe my parents were more French than inquisitive."

Ness frowned at that. "Alright. Yo, you Amiee. With an I-E-E. Better?" She nodded. "What can I do for you, Detective?"

"Did you see anything?"

"What could I see?" Amiee stretched like people do when they try to make themselves taller. "I can't see anything now and I'm here. When that happened, I was in there, and when I was in there, I was back against the wall behind the bar, and on the best of days when I'm feeling strong enough to wear my work heels, I still can barely see over it."

More sirens sounded outside. An ambulance stopped as close to the door as it could and a pair of EMTs jumped out. Once again, the door swished open and the EMTs lugging what looked like tackle boxes rushed in.

In an effort to be heard over the ever-increasing din, Ness shouted to Amiee. "Did anybody leave that room since I was there?" pointing at the lounge door. "Wait." Then turning toward the entrance Ness shouted, "Wait!"

Detective Ness intercepted the EMTs, saying whatever he said nearly directly into one's ear as the noise level ratcheted another notch higher. He gestured toward the elevator area and said something while standing in the lounge doorway. From what I could make out it sounded like, "...for sure, two men down. ... Four from Station 17. ... Duncan with them there too."

As the haze swallowed the EMTs Amiee spoke up. "Nobody went out or came in since your friend, Sgt. Duncan walked out of here with Marc, err, Mr. Crossley."

"What's that." The detective, still standing just outside the lounge doorway, turned back to face us. "Oh, yeah. Right. Okay, but don't go anywhere." His attention was drawn to someone coughing.

The smoke or dust or whatever it was was clearing and Sgt. Duncan stepped up beside his fellow officer. "We're going to need new morgue attendants." The sergeant coughed out. He was covered in a dusty soot that seemed to hover around him like a dirt cloud. "I'll call it in."

"What about the casualties?" Ness asked

"Yeah, we better get another ambulance here too. We're gonna need to check all them rooms down that hall and look for anybody else. Now, what do these two gotta say for themselves?" Duncan asked of his sidekick.

"The usual. Nobody saw nothing," Ness reported.

"Yeah, but then," Duncan wiped soot out of his eyebrows and turned to the hovering cloud of dust behind him, "in this case," he said hoarsely, "there really ain't much to see."

CHAPTER 7~ The Action Continued

The darkness of the night intensified with the storm.
Thunder cracked! Lightning flared! A shot rang out!
A piercing scream filled the air!
Large ships filled the small harbor.
The cannons' roar broke the morning calm!
The sides battled on.
Soon all was quiet even as the action continued

DUNCAN AND NESS WALKED back through the haze which had lifted enough that I could see the torn cage of the old elevator door hanging by the slimmest of slim metallic threads, and the blackened wall behind the elevator.

There was a lot of activity going on in front of that little wire enclosure and it was still noisy enough that it was like watching a silent movie. The two EMTs were kneeling on the floor in front of the elevator working on one of the morgue attendants. The other laid in a heap on the floor between them and what had once been the filigreed cage door. Two firefighters were inspecting the elevator shaft, pointing at something behind or under the cage itself. Off a little way, two more firefighters were knocking on doors going down the hall on the other side of the grand staircase to the right of the used-to-be elevator.

A quiet came over the lobby as the alarm finally was silenced and a person in full fire gear with ASST BAT CHIEF stenciled across the back of her coat walked through the now propped open door to join the growing crowd at the elevator site.

"Let's get out of here," I said to Amiee. "Nobody is coming back in here voluntarily any time soon."

"Sounds like a plan to me." Amiee fell in step next to me after having locked the door before I had half of that sentence spoken. "Your place this time. If she didn't join the crowd outside, Lily is still asleep on my bed. That poor girl. By the way, this is for you," she said as she handed me a paper wrapped breakfast sandwich.

"Aww," I said around inhaling the parcel. "I knew you loved me."

AS WE WALKED UP THE stairs I thought about how many times in the last day, the last twelve hours(!), I'd been up and down those stairs and through the upper hallway. Surely more than all the ten days I had been on site. It struck me with all those steps I took, I made little progress on my original mission. I was starting to wonder if I would ever get back to looking into whether the originals hanging on the walls of Hensley Manor were still originals, and if or how the Widow Hensley was involved.

"I'll meet you in your room. I want to check on Lily and grab something out of mine," and with that, Amiee scampered down the employee wing hall. I watched her little black skirted behind swinging down the hall and sighed.

I opened my room and flopped onto the bed. For it being barely ten in the morning, I was much too tired. I inhaled the aroma of the still warm package Amy pressed in my hand and then I rolled back off the bed. I pushed the single overstuffed chair closer to the desk and other chair against the side wall just as Amiee walked in bearing gifts. She had a coffee maker that uses those single serve pods, and a basket full of a variety of coffees in those very containers, ready to be turned into black gold.

"Oh my dear under-caffeinated doll! You really do love me!" Dropping my briefcase to the floor and pushing the art directory aside, I cleared the center of the desk. I then found two coffee cups in the alcove holding cups, glasses and an ice bucket and plopped those cups in the space I had just created.

"Well, we can talk about how you feel about me right now a little later." She batted those deep blue eyes at me. Was it my imagination or were her lashes longer this morning? As I pondered her makeup routine, she plugged in the machine, took the water holder section to the sink in the bathroom, filled it, and returned it to its spot on the side of the brewer. She popped a pod in place and pushed a couple of buttons. "If you really love me, you can offer me half of that sandwich."

Soon I was swooning to the aroma of Colombia's largest legal plant-based export and dividing the cook's contribution to breakfast in half, turning the single sandwich into two contributions.

"For right now right now, let's talk about what Lily told me," Amiee said as she took her half of the sandwich. She sat deep into the soft chair, tucking her legs under her and her hair behind one ear.

While we sipped our much too late morning eye openers, she went over how Lily and Lou had met, that they both also were interested in several pieces of art that had appeared at questionable auction sites, and had been "looking into things" for about two years now. They kept bumping into each other and would compare notes. "One day they compared themselves right to a justice of the peace and became Mr. and Mrs. G. Louis Vance."

"G. Louis?"

"G. Louis." She gave her head one sharp downward nod to confirm.

"So, the couple is a couple. Was a couple?"

"Indeed, a couple they are. Were. Whichever."

"Why the separate beds or was that too intimate a detail for her to go into?"

"It might have been too intimate, but I was curious enough to ask." Amiee interrupted herself to ask me, "Another cup? Same flavor?" I handed over my empty cup, and she did what she needed to do to turn it into a full cup. "So, she said he had real sensitive skin and if he touched hers, he'd break out like he had the chicken pox or something. That's also why he added essential oils to everything including his gun oil. She said he said that way he could take care of it and do whatever you do and not break out from using just plain oil."

"What did they do if they wanted to..." I pondered out loud.

"That I didn't ask. I figure to leave the lady a little dignity."

I sipped for a moment and thought for a minute. "He was born that way?"

"I don't know," Amiee said after swallowing a dainty bite of sandwich. "Lily said he said he had always been like that, but she got the impression something happened when he was a kid. It seems he didn't have much of a childhood. He spent the better part of it at some sort of home or hospital or facility." She paused a beat. "That's not right. It wasn't the better part of his childhood, but it was the bigger part. He couldn't go outside to play so spent most of his time inside reading and got interested in art at a young age. She also said he was smarter than he looked. He wanted to become a graphic designer but turned to art history instead. She also has a degree in art history and was working on some sort of book or magazine article when they met and like I said, they keep bumping into each other..."

"...as they were looking into things." I finished her sentence for her.

"Right," she said between a bite of sandwich and a sip of coffee.

"I wonder what she meant by looking into?" I mulled.

She prepared herself a second cup, then continued. "I didn't ask that either. I was just happy to find out that they aren't the bad guys."

"Just because they don't look like the bad guys doesn't make them the good guys. They still can be shady."

"For that matter Mr. Crossley, so can you. Just because you told me last night that you're working for some insurance company doesn't mean you are."

"But I showed you my papers."

"Yes, you did." She put her cup down. "How about showing me again. Please."

I reached down and lifted her in my arms, bringing her face to mine. I brushed my lips over hers on their way to her throat. I kissed her, running my tongue across her neck, kissing her here and there, slowly moving back, stopping when I reached her ear. I trapped her lobe between my teeth, and she sighed.

"Oh please, don't stop, don't ever stop." And I didn't until I did, and when I did, I stopped only long enough to lay her down and kiss her properly, or perhaps improperly. And there I will draw the curtains and let her retain her dignity. But trust me when I say the action continued.

CHAPTER 8~ Evening Fell

The darkness of the night intensified with the storm.
Thunder cracked! Lightning flared! A shot rang out!
A piercing scream filled the air!
Large ships filled the small harbor.
The cannons' roar broke the morning calm!
The sides battled on.
Soon all was quiet even as the action continued
The sun sank below the waves.

HOURS LATER, OR WHAT seemed like one rememberable lifetime later, we were back downstairs in the lounge. Dinner had just been served and the few guests who were still waiting for rides away from this house of horrors were drinking like there was no tomorrow, or so said my favorite bar maid.

Amiee had left my room sometime after noon. She went "home" and "freshened up" so she could open the lounge at 2:00. And here she was, freshened and in her work uniform sans blazer, with her hair pulled back into a short ponytail, exposing tiny ears with something different. Drop earrings terminating in a blue crystal, the same shade as her eyes that I now recognized as the same shade she tints the ends of her hair.

I had stayed behind in my room. After I cleaned up from our breakfast and post breakfast activity, I changed into my work uniform, khaki slacks with a red polo or golf shirt. I play neither so I'm never sure what to call shirts of that type. While I waited to go back to the first floor I made some calls, flipped through the directory of art at the Hensley, and made some notes. I brought my journal up to speed with what I knew or suspected to date. It was heavy on suspicion, light on knowledge.

As I slid onto my customary stool at the bar, I noted Lily was also at the bar, looking more composed than the last time I saw her. She was wearing the flowery sun dress Amiee thought would sort of fit her and it sort of fit her, although as suspected, a tad short for someone who had just lost her husband. I greeted Lily with a smile and a wave and Amiee with smile and an air kiss.

"Gawd, they're drinking like there's no tomorrow," Amiee managed to tell me while she paused between mixing up a pitcher of martini and pair of Manhattans. "What ever happened to a little whiskey on the rocks or a bottle of beer," she queried of no one in particular as she skewered two cherries on two swizzle sticks and dropped each stick into each Manhattan. "At least they're sticking to the classics. I don't know if I'm in shape for any Sex on the Beach," and winked at me with one of her ocean blue eyes. (And after I protected her dignity!)

Lily caught it and looked at me, then Amiee, then me, then Amiee, then, "Hmm." A pause, and then, "Well, as I was saying, Sgt. Duncan told me not to leave but said everyone else could go. I imagine the lounge will be pretty empty in another couple of hours." She turned to me. "Why are you sticking around, or is that a dumb question?" She was looking at me when her words came out but turned back to Amiee with a smile like women do when they know something.

Why am I staying I thought to myself. Because I've made diddly progress on why I'm here to begin with. Aloud I said, "Oh, I have reservations through the end of the month. I don't mind it being a little empty now. The way the public pays attention to current events, this place will be packed again by middle of next week." Lily's eyes dropped. Ooops. Poor word choice, and me supposed to be an up-and-coming novelist who should know a thing or two about word choice. "Oh, I'm sorry Lily. I didn't mean it to sound so flip. I just meant..."

"Don't worry about it," Lily said between sniffles. "I know you didn't mean anything by it."

"Oh good, the gang's all here." Detective Sergeant Duncan growled as he and Detective SomeKindOfGrade Ness plowed their way through the doors to the lounge. Duncan was carrying a cardboard mailing tube and a copy of the book of artwork hanging on the walls of the Hensley. "I'm glad to see nuttin' else got blowed up whilst we were off the premises. So who's here?" His eyes scanned the room, then he grumbled something to himself as he pointed the tube at each of us in turn. He aimed the tube to his partner. "Ness, go find Mrs. Hensley, that desk guy, and the maid. And see if the handy man ever turned up."

Ness left the lounge area while Duncan walked up to the bar. It probably had been my imagination, but I think we all took a step back at the same time. Maybe.

"Can I get you anything Sergeant?" Lilly moved over until she was across the bar from him.

"You know what I could go for? A Yoo-Hoo. You got any Yoo-Hoo?"

Amiee replied with a no in the textbook definition of deadpan. "Anything else, Howdy Doody?"

"Gimme a ginger ale."

A minor ruckus at the door caught everybody's attention. Ness pushed the Widow Hensley and Grayson into the room, then turned to chase somebody out the front door.

"I've never!" squelched the Widow

"See here now," said Grayson. With dignity of course.

"Well now, you two have a seat," Duncan carried his drink to one of the larger tables and stood next to it. "An' you three can come over too," he said over his shoulder to Amiee, Lily, and me.

"Thanks, but I'm needed behind the bar," Amiee said while measuring out the ingredients for a Boulevardier, "but I'm all ears. Well ... most of them." (I do believe she blushed, and I know Lily caught that one.)

Duncan swallowed down half of his ginger ale, looked at the glass like I look at a glass of bourbon when I'm looking for all the answers to life's questions, and started. "So we got a cause of death for Mr. Vance. Sorry ma'am." He aimed the last to Lily. "An' we're pretty sure we know what happened at the elevator. By the way, Jon Faithe, the morgue attendant who was injured, is in the hospital and doing okay." Murmured gratitude and relief ran around the table.

"You said you had a cause of death," I plowed in. "Some sort of poison?"

"Funny you should mention that seeing as how we all seen how he had a cord wrapped around his neck," and he tapped the cardboard cylinder for emphasis. "How did you steer your way down that road?"

"That wasn't a cord, or a rope, or a rolled-up pillowcase. It was canvas that someone twisted into that shape. I know paintings and I know canvas and I know you can't strangle someone with canvas. It would be like trying to stab someone with a cardboard knife. You'd think you can, canvas is just another type of material. You can use lots of different materials like a rope, but you'd never get a painted canvas to roll tight enough to get it strong enough to work like a rope."

"Very good for a mystery writer." There was something in the way he said 'mystery writer' that made me feel like I was playing the part of the emperor before a visit to his tailor. "That's right about the painting but how did you get to poison?"

Hmm. How did I without sounding like I knew before it happened. Which we all know I didn't! "Umm, a stab in the dark?" I stammered.

"Like with that cardboard knife probably. Well it kinda was and it kinda wasn't a poison." He finished off his ginger ale and looked into the glass before continuing. "It wasn't actually a poison but it is what it was that killed him." Again he turned to Lily, "Sorry ma'am," before finishing with, "He had an enormous amount of eucalyptus in his blood."

"Australia!" Amiee and I shouted together.

Duncan looked up at me, over to Amiee, then back to me. "I'm gonna let that go for now." Then he continued, "Oh, and the painting he had wrapped around him came from your room there Mr. Crossley."

"No. Wait. No! The painting in my room is there. The one in his room is missing!"

"And now how do you know that? That room's been locked up since this morning. Unless you knew it before we locked it."

Good point. "But. But. No. Wait." I thought I was done with one syllable words. "There is a painting in my room." I felt all eyes on me. I definitely was losing the room. "Amiee, tell them. There is a painting there. Really, there is"

"There's a painting in his room," Amiee shouted from behind the bar. "Really, there is."

"Don't bother alibiing his painting there, "he shouted over to Amiee, "We know it is. We also know it isn't." Now all eyes turned back to Sgt. Duncan. "There's a painting there but it ain't the right one. The painting hanging up in your room is some sunset. According to the book it's a ship on the horizon or something but all I see in it is a sunset."

"*Sailing Ship on the Horizon* by Henry Smith," I offered.

"Right," Duncan kept going. "But according to the book that's supposed to be in the Vances' room. This here one came out of your room." He tapped the cardboard tube again. "And this here one is the one the coroner unwrapped from around Mr. Vance's neck." And with that he opened the cardboard tube and slipped out a wrinkled canvas that opened to pastel seascape. I didn't have to look at the book to see what it said, but Grayson was already flipping through the book and read to us from the page where the work was reprinted.

Sunset on the Sea (alternatively *Sunset*), 1879
Pierre-Auguste Renoir, French, 1841-1919
Guest Room 205

Everyone gasped.

I gulped.

Amiee went, "uh oh."

"Uh oh is right Missy. Your boyfriend is in deep doodoo here. Yeah, we know. You should close your curtains." He aimed that one at me. (I thought I did close them. Wait! I know I did!)

"Wait a minute," Lily stepped in. "So far this has been a big reveal about how Lou wasn't killed. What about the eucalyptus? How did that kill him? He used it on everything. He even mixed it with his gun oil. He might as well have bathed in it."

"But it's toxic if taken internally." The eyes were all back on me. I couldn't have just sat there. No, I had to chime in.

"Very right again Mr. Mystery Writer." Okay, that time Duncan really did emphasize mystery and writer. "And according to the toxicology report, he had more eucalyptus in his system than your average koala bear."

"Actually, they aren't bears, they're marsup...uh." I stopped myself, wishing I hadn't said anything at all, but happy that I at least recognized I had a problem.

Lilly came over from the bar and plopped a bowl of cut lemons in front of me. "Next time you get the urge to open your mouth, stick one of these in there. Better still, I'll do it," and she sat down in the chair next to mine and pushed a yellow wedge between my lips.

"Apparently the stuff smells good—," Duncan began.

"Like Australia! That's why—" That time it was Amiee. "Sorry." She picked up a citrus wedge and sucked on it.

"Apparently the stuff smells good, but it causes convulsions, seizures, cuts off your breath, and don't do your heart no good if you drink the stuff." Duncan rushed through the explanation before he was interrupted again.

"But I have it in my tea all the time and I'm still here," the Widow Hensley, today in a mint green business suit, spoke up. I almost forgot she was in the lounge with us. "And what about my elevator?"

"The tea is just leaves steeped in hot water. It's not the oil. It's the oil you can't drink." The eyes shifted to Grayson. "I'm sorry. Did I say something wrong?"

A noise at the lounge entrance pulled all eyes to it. Ness stumbled through the door, panting like he had just run a marathon. "I couldn't catch him. It was the handyman." He fell into a chair and continued through heavy breaths. "It looks like he was heading for town, maybe. I couldn't tell for sure. I called in a BOLO on him. I never did find the maid."

"Yeah, maybe someone will spot him." Duncan thought but not for more than a second. "An' add the maid to lookout." To the Widow he said, "Let's hold that elevator talk for tomorrow. Now," he turned to me while pulling out his handcuffs. "Let's take this one in so it won't be a total waste of a trip out here."

Gasps sprung from everyone around the table.

"Take me in? Why?" I croaked.

"Because you're here," and he snapped the cuffs on.

"Amiee, there's my phone. Check the contacts, find my office, and tell them what's up."

"You got it. Wait. What's the passcode?"

"0-9-1-2"

"Hey! That's my birthday."

"I know."

"Wait. What?"

But I was already out of the lounge heading for the police car outside the door.

CHAPTER 9~ The Howling Dog

The darkness of the night intensified with the storm.
Thunder cracked! Lightning flared! A shot rang out!
A piercing scream filled the air!
Large ships filled the small harbor.
The cannons' roar broke the morning calm!
The sides battled on.
Soon all was quiet even as the action continued
The sun sank below the waves.
Somewhere a dog howled at the moon.

I WAS IN THE BACK OF the car with Ness, Duncan was in the passenger seat up front, and a young, uniformed officer was driving.

"Go ahead and take them off Elliot," Duncan said over his shoulder.

"Elliot?" I couldn't help myself.

Ness glared at me.

"Sorry. I'll shut up." And I did.

"It's Elwood. An old family name." Ness fumbled through his pockets before he pulled out a little key and fitted into the handcuff lock.

"Yeah. Like your old man didn't know what you'd end up putting up with in school. Why'd didn't you use your middle name or something? What is your middle name"

"Harrison."

"That's a good name. Harry Ness. I like it."

'Sure if it stayed Harry." Ness went on to explain. "My aunt, Uncle Harrison's second wife kept calling me what she called him and that's the one that stuck."

"Yeah, and?"

"Happy."

"So" Duncan unsuccessfully tried to hold back a giggle, "you were actually Mister Happy Ness!" and let loose with an honest to gosh belly laugh.

Ness struck back. "At least it's better than Sergeant No Name Duncan. I've been riding with you for two years and I still don't know your first name."

"Sure you do. It's Sargent. Like Sargent Shriver. My family was a big fan of the Kennedys but didn't want to be obvious about it."

Now Ness started to giggle. "If you ever get promoted, you'll be Lieutenant Sargent Duncan. Classy."

"Hey guys," I decided to risk not shutting up. "Remember me? What did we find out?"

Duncan turned as fully around as he could from the front seat. We hit a pothole and he bounced his head off the headliner. "Ow! Fingerprints wasn't useless but it was gonna to take an entire forensics team to get anythin' readable after he was blowed up in the elevator. We had enough of his DNA splattered all over the place to make a clone of him but unless he had a criminal record and that record involved somethin' that the arresting officer decided was worth getting a warrant for DNA, that wasn't gonna help neither. But we ran it through anyway. An' nothing come back. Then Elliot here..."

"Elwood."

"Then Mr. Happy Ness hisself here says let's try it on your requisition and we got a hit from a medical research project. I don't know what kind of pull you got but I'm glad you're on our side. So anyways, we now know who he really is."

"G. Louis Vance was an alias?" I was impressed and sounded so. "Good alias. Just enough detail to make it plausible." So, Amiee was right. They weren't who they said they were.

"Oh, G. Louis Vance is his real legal name." Ness picked up the narrative. "He had it legally changed about ten, twelve years ago." His birth name is...," he consulted his pocket notebook, "Gregory Louis van Rysselberghe, III."

I whistled lowly. "That makes his father Gregory Louis van Rysselberghe, II."

"That's the way it works the name numbering system," Happy, err, Elwood Ness chimed in.

"No. Listen to this," I said. "Gregory Louis van Rysselberghe, II is also known as 'Junior Van R,' is one of this year's most wanted on the Interpol's art crimes top ten."

Duncan took the reins again. "I don't know nothin' about no art criminals, but I know somethin' else. I know, our missing handyman didn't seem to exist before he started working at the inn. We pulled his DMV photo and sent it around and we got a hit from," he looked pointedly at me, "Interpol. They hadn't seen him for a while but confirmed he was known then as," now he flipped through the pages of his pocket notebook, "Gregory Louis van Rysselberghe, II."

I let out another low whistle.

Duncan continued, "So that makes him Louis II. And that makes him Louis III's daddy," he paused to look at Detective Ness, "because that's the way name numbers work out."

He looked happy with himself after that. For a short while. Then he turned on me, err, to me. "If you know this Van Rissle guy is your art criminal, how come you didn't recognize him?"

How come I didn't? "I never saw him. I mean I never saw him as Junior. To be honest, I started wondering if Junior was just made up so if something went wrong in your room they could say they'd send up Junior to take care of it. When I ran all my checks, their handyman was listed as Greg Berger. Nothing popped up on that name. Now I know why. This explains a lot."

"Wait," Ness entered the conversation "we know Vance is Louie III, which makes the erstwhile handyman of Hensley Manor, G. Louis Vance's daddy. Tell me Lou Three is some kind of criminal too like Lou Two."

"No. At least I don't think so." Did I really think so? "Amiee thinks the Vances are good guys. I thought it was just coincidence they showed up looking for the same thing I was assigned to investigate. But now..." I pondered for a half a beat. "No. They might not be the good guys, but they aren't the bad guys."

"Explain that," Ness asked of me.

I then went on to explain. "The van Rysselberghes are well known in the art world. Theophile van Rysselberghe was a Belgian post-impressionist influenced by Georges Seurat. His style evolved during his artistic career and most of his paintings were commissions that are still in private collections. He didn't drop out of sight, but he became increasingly private around 1910. Until his death in 1926 he lived a quiet life painting family members and sculpting. He had a distant cousin, Greogory, who felt he quit too early. He, Theo, was making money as an artist, something Gregory Van Rysselberghe never did. Rumor has it that Gregory began copying Theo's style after Theo moved away from Brussels. Gregory never did that well copying Theo's style, but he did much better when he switched to copying Theo's work. Then he began experimenting with copying other artists of all styles but did best with the impressionist and neo-impression schools. He had a son, Louis, that he worked with, grooming him to take over his growing counterfeit art business. Louis passed his talent to his son, Gregory Louis the First, and then keeping it in the family, G. Louis the Second, aka 'Junior Van R,' took over."

I wrapped it up with, "We never realized there was a G. Louis III. Well, there was, but it was thought he died as a small child when he was doused accidentally in cleaning solvent while playing in his father's studio." I paused there and remembered some of the things that Amiee told me that she had learned from Lily.

I looked out at the landscape as we drove past a cluster of trees thinking how at speed they look something like Theo Van Rysselberghe would have done if he did landscapes. "So that's why Lou was so interested in counterfeit art. I wonder. Did he know Junior was his father? Did Junior know Lou was his son?"

Duncan spoke up. "I don't know what Lou the Third knew but I'd said yes to that last question there. I'd say Berger knew about Vance but didn't want nobody else to know. You know?" He stretched a bit and turned around and began talking straight ahead to the inside of the windshield. "We've been wanting to talk to him since this morning, and he never seemed to be at the hotel there. When we checked with DMV for an address wouldn't you know, we actually found he has a trailer registered in his Berger name. We found it right where the registration said we would. We looked as much as we could around it and through the windows and found inside what looked like a bunch of art supplies, a couple air tank cylinders like what a diver wears, an' a compressor hooked up to what looked to me like a vacuum cleaner bag."

"Ah. So now I see the dust is settling." I mused.

"Very funny." Duncan almost laughed again. "Where you want to spend the night? In the drunk tank?"

"With that pack of dogs. No thank you. Take me to the Four Seasons. I can use a night of luxury."

"Hmm." Duncan had close to a glint going in his eye as far as I could tell from the back seat. "I'd think you'd have rather had a night in—"

I stepped in before he could finish. "Leave that curtain closed, please."

Now it was time for Ness to chime in. "What's your office gonna tell her when she calls," making air quotes around office.

"Very adult," I sneered. "They'll explain I have some sort of immunity, and that they trust in my judgement, and that I've been a loyal agent and thus and such, and that they'll have me out in the morning, and then that will be that."

Ness nearly jumped across to seat at me. "And you let her worry and wonder what all that means while you spend the night at the Four Seasons. Ain't you ashamed of yourself doing that to those girls? They didn't do nothing"

"Girls?"

"I mean girl," Ness stammered.

"Uh huh. Well, actually, no, I'm not ashamed. Not at all." I leaned back in my seat as much as I could lean back in the back seat of a police car. "Because about five minutes after that call, she'll get another call from my office saying I have to see her right away and someone is waiting at the front door to drive her downtown. And there will be someone, and they will go downtown. To the Four Seasons. I'm sure after the initial confusion, she'll enjoy her night of luxury too."

"You're back to Elliot,' Duncan spoke to Ness. "We just found ourselves a new Mr. Happiness."

CHAPTER 10~ A New Dawn Broke

The darkness of the night intensified with the storm.
Thunder cracked! Lightning flared! A shot rang out!
A piercing scream filled the air!
Large ships filled the small harbor.
The cannons' roar broke the morning calm!
The sides battled on.
Soon all was quiet even as the action continued
The sun sank below the waves.
Somewhere a dog howled at the moon.
The sun rose abruptly!

I LOOKED AROUND THE room and marveled at how neat it was. Nothing seemed out of place. The bathroom look like nobody had used it which I knew was not the case, being one who had indeed used it. Amiee's bag was neatly stacked and waited patiently on the bag tender. I felt ashamed for even thinking about it.

"I followed you all the way to the air tanks and vacuum bag. What's that all about?" Lily asked between sips of caffeine paradise. Literal paradise.

With sunlight streaming through the southeast facing windows of our suite, we were enjoying a room service breakfast of classic Eggs Benedict, fruit cups of fresh berries with golden kiwi, a generous pitcher of orange/pineapple/mango juice, and a pot of hot coffee brewed from a blend of beans grown in Hawaii's famous Kona coffee region after a night of... well, it gave us an appetite for a big breakfast.

"Remember when Duncan told those first responders that there was no fire, and all that smoke was mostly dust?"

She interrupted "That was Ness."

"Was it? Doesn't matter. Someone said it was mostly dust. When I heard whoever it was say that."

"Whomever?"

I thought a minute, "You know what? I don't know." I sipped my coffee and still didn't know. "Well, whichever it is, when I heard somebody say it was mostly dust, at the time I didn't think anything of it. Then when Duncan said they found metal cylinders and a bag of dust, at Berger's," I stopped myself at her puzzled look. "I mean at Junior's, it all fell into place." Another sip of coffee. "Oh, this coffee is delicious. We should see if we can buy a bag from them."

"You do that, Agent Crossley, and then we can discuss custody." Amiee tapped the rim of her cup. "Back to the dust."

"Right. Back to the dust. Wait. I'm sorry. I have to ask this. Why is this place so freaking neat?"

Amiee calmly sipped her coffee. "What do you think I was doing while you were calling for this most excellent breakfast? I can't stand anything out of place. Now, about the dust."

"Right. Back to the dust. Wait. I've been in your room and a picture of it would not be in the dictionary under 'neat.'"

"You only saw the sitting room. That's the decompression room. The bedroom is not neat as a pin but as neat as I keep the bar. You can't say that a mess. Now, about the dust."

"Right. Back to the dust. Wait" I couldn't stop myself. "I've been in your bedroom. Last night. When we, you know."

"No, we didn't"

"We didn't? We sure as what I know I remember we did, do. Did. Didn't we?"

"Not in the bedroom."

I was so confused. "No?"

"Nope. We never left the love seat."

"Oh. Aptly named too." She smiled at that.

"And that actually was day before yesterday, or very, very early yesterday. Yesterday yesterday we were in your room. Now," Amiee said firmly, but still smilingly, "about the dust. And by the way, we didn't do you know in my place. We just snuggled. On the loveseat."

"Right. Sorry about that. Two nights ago. Hmm." I cleared my throat. "Well now, about the dust." I finished off that cup and refilled it with hot coffee from the pot. "What you do is you blow dust particles into a tight cylinder until it's about three quarters full, then fill the rest of the space with compressed air so the dust is suspended throughout the tank. If you can ignite a dust particle, the whole thing explodes like a bomb with a bang but no fire, all the energy goes to blowing the tank apart rather than burning. Berger set the tanks—"

"Berger, Schmerger." Amiee set her cup down and had her hand poised over the pot. She shook her head and said, "Can't we just call him Junior so I don't have to translate in my mind?"

"Right. Junior set the tanks at the bottom of the elevator shaft and fashioned a contact detonator using a spring switch, steel wool, and a watch battery. All he needed was a spark at the valve and the dust in the tank would ignite and the compressed air would blow the tank apart. When the car got close to the ground floor landing, the bottom of it compressed the springs, closed the circuit with the battery, created that needed spark, and boom," I spread my arms for emphasis, "the dust bomb exploded. All the injuries were due to flying debris, not heat or fire. Or at least not enough heat or fire to cause much damage." I looked at my coffee cup like it held all the answers to life's questions. "Can it really just be the beans? I bet they have some sort of super coffee brewer to make it this good."

"Wait a minute." Amiee still looked puzzled. "If there wasn't any fire, what happened to Lou's fingerprints. I thought his hands were burned."

I set my cup back on the table. "They were. I don't think that was planned but here's what I think must have happened. When Lily went in to take her shower, Junior stopped by to reacquaint himself with his son. At this point, I don't know if he knew if Lou knew who Junior is,.. was? ... but Junior did know, or at least strongly suspected, that Lou was close to fingering him as the counterfeiter. So, son or not, Lou had to go. It was easy for him to get into the room. Knock on the door and say he needed to change a bulb, check a bad outlet, or do something custodial. While Lou wasn't looking, Junior spiked his water with eucalyptus. Then he just had to wait a couple minutes for it to do its thing, set the stage, and vamoose."

"Set the stage?" Amiee asked with a puzzled look on her face.

I went on. "Junior was going to frame me by switching the painting in the room. He just finished watching Lou take his last breath and got the painting from my room around Lou's neck when the shower stopped. He knew Lily would be out soon and he wanted out of there. In his haste, he must have spilled some of the oil and Lou's hands were still covered in it when he took his last elevator ride. When the tanks blew, there was just enough heat from the initial spark and flash to make the oil combust and bye bye fingerprints."

Amiee took all this in. "Then Junior knows who you are, and he was going for a twofer by framing you?"

"I don't know. He might have. Or he might have picked me because I'm the only other guest who's been there longer than just a couple days and figured I'd still be around when the cops figured out what was wrapped around Lou's neck."

Amy leaped up from her chair. The coffee cup crashed and splintered into pieces as it hit the floor. "Oh no! No no no! If Lou was close to accusing Junior and Junior knew that, and Lou and Lily had been working together, and Junior knows that too, that means Lily is still in danger! We've gotta warn her!" Amiee was already getting dressed while she was still talking.

"Oh damn! You're right! Why hadn't I thought of that?" I started pulling clothes on too.

I reached for my phone and called the office. "We need a car to get back to the Hensley and we need it like yesterday! We're not waiting." I was frantically stuffing our few last items in the suitcase. "Tell whoever you get to pick us up on the road between here and there. We'll be the ones running like we stole something. Wait! Before you call transportation, get on the phone to the Hensley and warn Lily Vance that she is in danger and not to leave her room. And tell her not to let anybody in except me or Amiee." Some of that I said while we were already pounding down the stairwell.

We flew through the Four Seasons lobby and out to the street. We turned east and raced along the roads the two miles it would take to get from lobby to lobby. At about the half mile point a standard issue black SUV pulled in front of us, the back door opened, and we piled in.

"Buckle up folks." The driver said and he slammed the big truck back into gear and took off with a chirp of his tires spinning against the pavement. "This is going to be the fastest mile and a half since Secretariat ran at the Belmont."

We barely had time to catch our breaths when while racing down the highway the Hensley rose in front of us, the sun looking like a giant yellow ball hovering over its roofline. It grew larger as the SUV's big engine grew louder.

Just then, light as bright as that sun itself flashed, and when we could see again, we were seeing the front of the Hensley in flames.

"Holy crap! What was that?" That was the driver.

"Oh, that's not good." That was me.
"You really know how to show a girl a good time."

CHAPTER 11~ "Snow" Falls

The darkness of the night intensified with the storm.
Thunder cracked! Lightning flared! A shot rang out!
A piercing scream filled the air!
Large ships filled the small harbor.
The cannons' roar broke the morning calm!
The sides battled on.
Soon all was quiet even as the action continued
The sun sank below the waves.
Somewhere a dog howled at the moon.
The sun rose abruptly!
Snow fell across the land.

WE BOUNCED IN OUR SEATS as the big SUV jumped onto the sidewalk and screeched to a stop.

"Oh man I hope Lily ignored us and left her room." I said as we jumped out of the truck across the street from the blazing façade. I was already halfway across the street when I had that thought.

As we pounded our way across the street in the shadow of the building, Amiee was right beside me. "Do you have any idea how we're going to get through that?" she gasped between breaths. "That's like the proverbial wall of fire only it's a literal wall of fire."

"I'm thinking." I said that but I can't say what I was thinking. This was bad. Very bad.

"You better think fast because this street isn't that wide and like, here we are!"

And then I stopped thinking and let instinct take over

"Around back!" and I turned to the right to circle the building, Amiee at my side, still lock-stepped with me.

We got around to the pool deck and ground to a halt when we saw people already there.

"It looks like they evacuated to here." I breathed out between pants.

I scanned the crowd. The Widow Hensley, Grayson, a couple handful of Hensley employees in a few clumps, and, and, and ... no Lily. No Greg Berger either, although I suppose he could have been one of the random employees milling around the pool. He could be any one of the people on the patio. I still had never seen him. Nobody looked guilty although I'm not sure what guilty might have looked like at that point. This could be a classic example of hiding in plain sight. Still, I continued to look for, for... for what? For a sign to pop up over someone's head? What we needed now was an arrow pointing out the guilty party or parties, or someone to jump up and say 'It was me! I did it.'

Considering the building right next to them was doing its best to audition for next sequel to Raging Inferno, this crowd seemed surprisingly calm. Too calm. Happy even. People were in small and larger groups, chitting and chatting. Some were even holding plastic glasses and laughing and smiling.

"Amiee. What does Junior look like?" I asked as I kept scanning the clusters of people.

Together we focused on the people around the pool. "I don't know that I could describe him," Amiee said as she looked here and there. He's pretty plain in a dull sort of way. I could pick him out of a crowd though."

I pointed to the growing mass of people around the pool deck. "Well, check out that crowd and tell me if he's there to be picked."

She scanned the group of people in maid, kitchen, and custodial uniforms. "No, not with the other employ— wait! That's him!" she pointed to the opposite side of the pool by the property line fence. "Talking to Grayson. The guy in gray overalls."

I zeroed in on the one she indicated and took off running from a dead stop. Over my shoulder I shouted back to her, "You look for Lily! If she's not here, find Sgt. Duncan. He's probably on his way if he heard the call. If you don't see him, call the station and have them find him. I'm going after Berger," and continued running across the patio.

The movement must have caught his eye because Berger pushed Grayson away, dropping him into the pool with a splash, and then he took off toward the far side of the building.

"Help!" Grayson gasped out, bobbing in water. The crowd surged toward the flailing manager, blocking my way to the sprinting Berger.

I broke free of the crowd just as he reached the corner of the building.

"Berger!" I scream after him. "Stop! Stay where you are!" (Hey, it works in the movies.)

He ran faster and disappeared around the corner. I chugged around the same corner and saw ... nothing. No Berger. Where did he go? I slowed to a walk and checked out the side of the building.

As near as I could remember, the other side of this wall was the banquet room. There were no outside entrances to it. On the inside, the wall was basically one big window. No doors in it that I remembered. And although the building isn't very large, he could not have run all the way to the front in the little time it took me to get to the corner. I should be seeing him. Odd. I also should be seeing flames or smoke or something and saw none of that either. Nor did I see any firefighters or hear any fire trucks or equipment. Except for some crowd noise filtering around from the pool behind me, it was all calm. Too calm. As I neared the far end of the wall, I slowed to a walk and thought about this. It was like there was no explosion, there was no fire, and there never was. But I saw it. We saw it.

I reached the front corner of the building, breathing close to normal now fully recovered from my sprint along the side of the building. I turned to the front and saw a perfectly plain, unburned, unsooty, could maybe use a coat of paint but otherwise un-unusual looking building. How could that be? And what was I walking on. It looked like snow. Like some kind of theatrical prop snow but lighter.

I heard footsteps running up behind me and I turned to see my driver jogging toward me. "The lady said you came around this way."

"The lady knows."

"Right. After I saw you go around the other side of the building, the fire," he made air quotes when he said fire, "went out. Or rather turned off. Or something." He just ran all the way around the same building I had just run only a quarter of the way around. Why didn't he sound out of breath?

He went on, "I was already on with dispatch to get the fire department when it just stopped. Like poof. I 86'd the fire department and had them find Sgt. Duncan and Detective Ness, then waited out front until they showed up. They're around back with your lady friend."

"Thanks," I said, still struggling to figure how someone staged such a conflagration. "Hey. While you were waiting on Duncan and Ness, did you see anybody come or go, or anything that didn't look right?"

"Besides something just turning off a raging inferno?"

"Yeah, besides that."

"No sir." He shook his head for emphasis. "No one, no thing. Sorry."

"Yeah, that's okay. Thanks again." I think I mumbled it more than I said it. That was because I had bent down and was concentrating on the white ash looking stuff laying all around. "You said it just stopped. Like poof."

"Yessir. Poof. Just stopped. Sir?" The young driver had my attention again. "Sir. What is that stuff?"

"Nitrocellulose. Or what's left after you burn it." And I ran my fingers through a pile of dry, white flakes.

"Nitro what sir?"

"Never mind," I straightened up and turned around to start back to patio, but then turned back and said to the driver, "Stay on the street here and don't let anybody leave from the front door or from that sidewalk over there," indicating the side opposite where I had just come. "Nobody. And call the police department. See if they can send a couple guys to post up by the patio and pool." I trotted around the way I had come, past the banquet hall windows and back onto the pool deck.

A VERY WET GRAYSON saw me and came up to me in as much a snit as he could muster while still dripping wet. "What were you doing, charging around here like some nut?" he sputtered. "And why were you chasing Junior? And why did he push me into the pool?"

"What were you guys talking about while the building was burning?" I asked him.

"Burning!" The Widow cried out, leaping out of her poolside chaise. Today she was in a hunter's green maillot with sun yellow sandals and wrapped in a floral cover up. "Now what have you done to my building?"

"You're not all out here because of the fire?" I asked, adding my own air quotes.

"What fire? What are you talking about?" The Widow needed to calm down. She was getting as red as her hair. "We're out here because it's Cook's birthday and she made a buffet breakfast to celebrate. There are no guests left thanks to you and those Vance creatures." She paused to take a breath and to let some of her venom for those of us who remained sink in. "Cook said Junior had suggested it and she thought, and I agreed, that this would be a good boost for everybody. Now what fire?" She started sort of calmly but by the time she finished, she was back to squelch level.

Just then, Sgt. Duncan walked over to us and started in before I could answer the Widow. He jumped in with, "So Amiee tells me you had some excitement this morning. But she didn't tell me why I'm out here at sunrise responding to a fire that isn't there!" Duncan was doing his best impression of a non-morning person.

"What fire!?" Grayson joined the Widow in synchronized squelching.

Amiee who had stepped up from somewhere and stood next to me now stepped into the conversation. "When we pulled up the street, we saw the flash of an explosion and the whole front of the budding was on fire. There was a fire. We both couldn't have imagine it. We three! The driver saw it too!" And now even she was approaching squelch volume. "There were three of us who saw it. You can't tell me that three, three," three fingers up and waving for emphasis, "three people could have imagined the same thing!" She took a breath, calmed herself, and turned to speak to me. "Sgt. Duncan said it was out by the time he pulled up."

"Not out, missy," Duncan growled. "Ain't never was."

"Yes, there was, and I'll show you," I jumped back in. "But right now we have to find Berger and Lily. Amiee, did you ever find her out here?"

"No, I was just getting ready to check inside when these two showed up."

"Okay. Take Ness and go check her room." I asked Duncan, "Is that okay with you?"

"Yeah, yeah," he grumbled in reply.

"Okay," I turned back to Amiee, "you two check for Lily upstairs." Then I turned to Duncan. "Sarge, you come around front with me. I want to show you something. And Amiee," I shifted to her again as she and Ness opened the glass doors. "Be careful. Berger, err, Junior is still running free somewhere."

"We will, Hon." She gave me a little finger wave and air kiss.

As the two of them disappeared into the rear of the building, I turned back to Sgt. Duncan. "You're going to want to see this."

I paused and thought for a second, then shouted over what I now knew to be a crowd of partying employees, "Happy birthday, Cookie!"

WE WALKED TO THE FRONT the way I had gone when I chased Berger from the pool deck. I showed Duncan where I figured he had gotten to by the time I got to the back corner on my short chase. "He couldn't have gone much farther than this. I don't see how he could have vanished." We continued along the building to the street side that was on 'fire.' "But I don't see how a three-story building can be on fire one minute and intact the next. Until I saw this." I showed him the piles of flaky white ash. "It doesn't help me find our missing suspect, but it does explain the missing fire." I bent down and gathered some into the palm of my hand.

"What's that?" he wanted to know.

"Nitrocellulose. Flash paper." I held my hand up to my face and puffed at the flaky white material into the air. "The stuff magicians use to make something go poof in a cloud of smoke. Probably flash cotton actually. Several sheets of it ignited in series, the last couple treated with something to burn slower or maybe plain cotton so it looks like a real fire. Between the sunlight just coming up behind the building and the flash of the initial ignition, it looked like an explosion without the sound. We didn't notice that there was no sound because we were still coming up the block. Now that I think about it, we weren't all that far away. We should have heard the boom of a real explosion. I paused for a beat to think about that. "We saw the flash but didn't hear a boom. Or even a loud whoosh. That much flash paper would have to make a good whoosh." I shook my head in thought. "No, we were too far away for that. Now that I am thinking more clearly, even inside the SUV, we would have heard a boom if there had been a boom to hear. No. there was no explosion and no real fire. Just the whoosh of all that flash paper doing what magicians have used it for over centuries. Causing a distraction."

"If a building catches fire and nobody is in the woods, does it make a sound," Duncan mused.

I shuddered at that. "But this isn't the woods, and we were there to see it," and pointed to the black SUV still half on the sidewalk across the street. "There was a fire but then there wasn't. No boom, no fire. Just that flash. When we got here whatever he used to slow things down was flaming but it already must have been burning out. We didn't know that because Amiee and I went straight around to the back. There is where we saw Berger and I took off after him."

"So you figure he did this?"

"The Widow told me the little gathering out back was his idea. It looked like he wanted them around back and the fire," using those air quotes again, "would distract anybody left inside or keep anybody from coming into the building through the main entrance while he snatched Lily. Which it did because that's where we were going."

"Good theory except according to your story, he was out back joining the festivities while the fire was burning itself out." Duncan was rubbing his chin like people do when they're deep in thought. "If he was using this as a distraction he'd have been inside where the Vance lady is and they'd have been somewhere to watch the street to make sure nobody was coming in." Now it was Duncan's turn to mull things over. "No. It wasn't him. Or it was him with an accomplice." He looked around at the white ash at our feet. "I thought that magic paper stuff didn't leave no ash. Why are we seeing all this? It looks like it just snowed here."

"I don't know. I guess because he used so much it accumulated. Maybe he started with flash paper and added something else to make flames. This ash could be cotton or canvas. But it looks like snow, does it it? It reminds me of *Snow Scene at Moret*, by Alfred Sisley. Odd thing about Sisley. He was a British citizen, but he was born and died in France."

"Art people." He sneered like he said 'mystery writer' the day before. "C'mon. Let's go see if your girlfriend dug up the other girl."

CHAPTER 12~ Dancing in the Garden

The darkness of the night intensified with the storm.
Thunder cracked! Lightning flared! A shot rang out!
A piercing scream filled the air!
Large ships filled the small harbor.
The cannons' roar broke the morning calm!
The sides battled on.
Soon all was quiet even as the action continued
The sun sank below the waves.
Somewhere a dog howled at the moon.
The sun rose abruptly!
Snow fell across the land.
They danced madly in the garden.

I TURNED TO WALK BACK around the way we came when Duncan stopped me. "Let's be daring and walk through the wall of fire."

"Huh?"

"The front door," he said pointing to the main entrance. "We don't gotta go chasing all around the outside again. Let's take the front door like normal people." As we approached the front door he added, "An' will you lookit here. Here comes the cavalry."

A marked car pulled into the circle and two uniformed officers stepped out. "Geez, could they spare all the both of yinz. Go 'round back and don't let nobody leave that party they got going on. Crossley's man here is watching the front."

As we walked through the doors into the lobby I took a visual inventory. Lounge to the right, grand staircase ahead and to the right, service hallway to the kitchen and other service areas just right of the stairs, former ornate cage elevator straight ahead, reception desk ahead and to the left, and banquet room, as it's always been, to the left along the north wall. I turned left.

"Let's go there. I want to check something out," and walked to the pair of burled walnut doors separating the banquet hall from the entrance lobby.

But for the outside wall, the room looked like it had just been the subject of photo shoot celebrating mid-century ballroom design. The room had been created by combining the sitting room, a parlor, and a dining room when the building was a private residence. It stretched almost the depth of the building, a perfectly proportioned three to two rectangle. Plush carpet, old timey floral looking wallpaper, chandeliers that looked a lot like crystal exactly every ten feet, perfectly centered between the long walls. No tables or chairs were set up. Just a big empty room. Against the short wall farthest from the doorway where we stood, the carpet was replaced with parquet flooring to create a dance area. Hanging against that wall the Renoir's 1886 masterpiece, *Dance at Le Moulin de la Galette.*

Across the room, directly opposite from where we stood was a wall of glass. All glass. Not all in one piece. Ten ten-foot-wide panes made up that wall of glass. Must have been a bear to keep clean and it was clean. Not a streak, not a smudge. But. "There. What's that?" I asked half to myself and started across that soft carpet intent on a spot I spied.

"What do you got in your sights?" Duncan queried.

"He hid in plain sight before. Maybe he's at it again," I said. "Or maybe not so plain this time."

"What are you talking about?" Duncan asked as he followed in my wake across the room.

"Berger had to have come in here and the only way in is through that glass."

Duncan held up his hand and started tapping the tips of his fingers with the finger of his other hand, "So far this guy has been an art forger, a pyrotechnic genius, and a magician's assistant."

"Let's not forget murderer," I added.

"I'm getting to that. Murderer. And now you think he's Casper the ghost and can walk through glass walls. And I'm out of fingers!" (My, how people like to squelch!)

"Not through glass. Around glass." I reached for the spot we had been walking to. We were now in the corner diagonally from the corner where we walked in. On the floor in front of us, set into the wood trim separating the carpet from the wood floor, turning the dancing section into an island of wood within the plushness of the carpet, deep into the corner nearly up against the short wall beyond the last piece of glass and the back wall, was a small brass button. I hovered my foot over it, nodded toward the windows, then pressed down.

The second pane from the right, but for a soft hum, slid soundlessly over the pane to its right.

"Open sez-a-me," Duncan deadpanned.

I rolled my eyes at him.

We walked through the opening and turned toward the back of the building. "I bet they intended this to be some sort of outside extension to the ballroom and haven't gotten around to developing it yet. There must be a way in from the outside like what's in there, and that's how Berger performed his disappearing act." I started feeling my way along the outside wall between the glass panel and the rear corner of the building. The building was an old mansion, built from the type of gray stone that was used to build most brownstones. Big blocks of stone held together with a nice crisp mortar line between courses.

"It has to be on this wall. It wouldn't be in the ground, that wouldn't make sense. That area ultimately would be covered by cement or some type of paving. And it wouldn't be at the front corner. If it was there, he'd have still been in sight when I came around that corner." I swiveled my head from the front to the back of the building. "There's about ten feet of wall from this last pane to the back corner and I'll bet your paycheck it's somewhere on this wall around eye level."

"If you win that bet it ain't gonna be lining your pockets with gold, but I'll buy you and your girlfriend dinner. Hey!" He was running his fingers along the mortar line when he stopped, "I think I just doubled my pay from this week. Lookit here."

He had indeed found a raised spot almost the exact shade of gray as that of the mortar. He pushed it and nothing happened.

"Well don't that make no sense. It's a button that don't do nothing. Like my garage door opener half the time." He stared at it, willing it to do something.

"Hmm. Maybe..." I reached over and pushed it twice. The glass pane began moving in the opposite direction. When it was completely closed, I reached for it again and pressed it one time. The pane began to slide to its open position. Two more button presses and it closed, One more and it opened again. "One to open. Two to close."

"Now that we done that dance, let's go find your girlfriend."

WE WALKED THROUGH THE opening again, this time to the inside. I stepped to the corner where I stepped on the brass switch twice and the window closed. Then we stepped our way to the lobby. And we stepped right into a squirming Amiee and my driver, the driver holding her arms behind her in the position you expect someone to be in while snapping on a set of handcuffs. Except our drivers don't carry handcuffs. Even as Amiee struggled, she couldn't break his grip.

"Marc! Tell him to let me go." Amiee squelched.

"It's okay. Let her go. What made you—"

"Lily's gone!" Amiee squelched. Again.

Sgt. Duncan jumped in. "Where's Ness?" to Amiee. Then to the driver, "An' why are you still holdin' her? Let her go already," Then back to Amiee, "Okay your turn to dazzle me with a story. Go."

"Lily's gone. And Detective Ness is gone too! We came in like you said and went up the back stairs," Amiee began. "At the top of the stairs, two maid's carts were tied together and tied to the tops of the railings to block off the hall from the stairs." She stopped long enough to shake her head back and forth. "No, no, they weren't tied. Not tied like with rope or string or even a sheet. They were chained in place. We didn't have anything that could cut through it and wouldn't want to take the time if we did, so we climbed over them. We worked our way over, but it took forever. Did you ever try climbing up onto and over something with wheels?" She stopped for a beat or two to catch her breath, then continued, "Anyway, we finally got over them and headed for her room. When we get to her room, the door was open and the room is empty, but we heard something from the employee wing.

"We ran through the upper lobby to the other hall. By now, Detective Ness is pretty far in front of me and he gets there first." She stopped and shuddered. "I can still hear her screaming."

"You sure it was her?" Duncan queried.

"I know it was her. I remembered her scream" Then Amiee continued, "When I got into the hall, I saw Ness going into the linen closet. I followed him and I don't know what I was thinking but I said to myself, I'm going in after them. But the door was locked. I didn't even know that door had a lock. The ones in the guest wings do but I never knew this one locked too. We just always went in ourselves to get what we need."

After another breath Amiee went on. "I banged on the door but didn't get anything for it and as near as I could tell, I couldn't hear anything through it either. So that was when I came down here to look for you two.

"I wasn't going to fight with the blocked back stairs, and I knew you'd be out front anyway," she took another deep breath. "I came down the main stairs and out the front door and that's when this one grabbed me." She wrapped up by glaring at the driver who was still standing behind her, looking ready to contain and control.

"Sir, you said not to let anybody come out this way. Sir." The driver looked as nonplussed as one could, assuming one knew how to look nonplussed. "Sir, I know she's with you sir, but you said nobody, and nobody means no body, so I stopped her."

Just then, Detective Ness walked into the lobby from the hall next to the main staircase, looking disheveled like he knew how to look disheveled.

"Elwood Ness! Where did you come from and geez, Louise, what the hell happened to you?" Duncan called across the lobby.

"Elwood?" Amiee asked.

"Later," I answered.

"This one here," Duncan said while pointing to my unofficial assistant, "just told me you was locked in a closet. Now how'd you get here, and where are the other two you was chasing after?" Duncan asked.

"If I ever see them again, I'll be sure to ask them. They better not hurt that girl is all I have to say."

"They?" Duncan queried.

"Yeah. Two of them. Has to be. Two of them plus Mrs. Vance." And now Ness began his tale. "I chased them, Berger carrying Lily, Mrs. Vance down the hall and spotted him ducking behind a door. I got there before it closed and had barely got through the door when somebody hit me across the back of my head. It had to be someone else standing to the side waiting for me to come in. I dropped…" He winced at the memory. "I dropped hard and when I came to it was dark.

I sort of reached around and couldn't feel anything on the floor with me. Or for what it was worth, I couldn't feel anybody either. I felt the wall alongside the door and found a light switch and flipped it.

"The room was your basic looking linen closet. Lots of sheets, towels, and little soaps and shampoos but no Berger and no girl. So I let myself out. Or was going to. I turned the knob and nothing happened. I figured it was locked and turned the little button, only it's not a button. You know the thing in the middle of the doorknob you turn to lock and unlock the door?" We nodded. "Well, I turned it, and when I did, the shelf behind me slides into the wall and there's these stairs there.

Ness took a breath then continued, "A skinny spiral staircase. I wasn't getting out the door and I figured that's where they went so that's where I went. It bottoms out in the kitchen inside the walk-in cooler which was a lot easier to get out of than the linen closet.

"I went out the back and I see there's two of our men back there, so I check with them if they saw anybody come out of the building. They said nobody came out that way, so I turned myself around and came out this way."

Duncan turned to the driver. "You didn't see nobody else come out the front entrance before this here lady."

"No sir."

"Well, where the hell did they go?" Duncan squelched at his loudest and threw his arms in the air! "He ain't no magician's assistant. He's frigging Houdini hisself!"

"I know where he went," I said confidently. And then less confidently, "I think I know. I think he went to his trailer."

"And how did he get there? Fly off the roof?" Duncan was squelching again.

"No. I think he walked right out the building. And danced right around us while he did.

CHAPTER 13~ A Horse Bucked

The darkness of the night intensified with the storm.
Thunder cracked! Lightning flared! A shot rang out!
A piercing scream filled the air!
Large ships filled the small harbor.
The cannons' roar broke the morning calm!
The sides battled on.
Soon all was quiet even as the action continued
The sun sank below the waves.
Somewhere a dog howled at the moon.
The sun rose abruptly!
Snow fell across the land.
They danced madly in the garden.
A horse bucked while pulling the wagon.

"GEEZ LOUISE! YOU MEAN you really is being some kind of Houdini. Or maybe he's the invisible man this time." I'd say here that the good sergeant was squelching again, but it was more accurate to say 'still' because he never came down from that pitch.

"Hold on there Sarge and hear me out." I began my theory. "I figured he took those stairs into the kitchen and out into the banquet hall."

"He can go there from there? I don't remember seeing no doors in that room besides the big wood doors over here" Duncan asked while pointing to the large double doors we had just used to go in and out of the banquet hall.

"Sure he can." Amiee explained, "A banquet hall that can't be accessed by a kitchen wouldn't be much use in the banquet business. Mr. Hensley had a bunch of doors that didn't look like doors put in when he built the ballroom and commercial kitchen. He hated to break the line of a wall. Anyway, that back wall has a panel that slides away so it looks like one complete wall when it's closed. But when it's open there's access to the kitchen, a bus station, beverage station, even a small bar that I've used for some functions. You wouldn't know that's all there unless you were in the room when we have something going on and we were all set up for it."

"And Berger would have known about it and how to open it just like he did to get the glass panel open," I said as I regained control of the conversation. "He got into the banquet hall and then he slipped through the window-door while we were out front checking out the ashes. I'd guess he got to the corner just as we were coming in the front door. He probably was ready to make a break for it when he spotted that one," I indicated the driver, "so he was going to go back inside the way he came out. But when he, Berger, saw him, the driver, rush into the building to stop her," I tapped Amiee on her shoulder, "he, Berger, saw his chance and made a dash for wherever his vehicle was stashed."

"Employees park in the lot across the street," Amiee volunteered.

"He sees my driver nab Amiee coming through the door then bring her back inside. That's his chance so he takes it and lams out of here. Had it not been for her trying to come out the front door, Berger might have figured he was trapped. Maybe he might have even considered turning himself in. I'm guessing he still has Lily because we haven't found her anywhere else yet. Maybe she's gagged. Maybe she's unconscious and he's carrying her all this time. Neither way can be too easy for him to handle alone so I think he still has his mystery accomplice with him too. The logical place for them to go would be the trailer. I think we'll find him, Lily, and at least one other person with him." I took a deep breath and let that all sink in.

"Okay. I can buy all the running downstairs and through walls and windows but what makes the trailer such a logical place?" Duncan wanted to know.

"You said he had art supplies there. What?" I asked, "Canvases, paints, stretchers?"

"Yeah, that an' some easels, drop cloths, brushes, n'at. All like regular art studio stuff. And lots of solvents and other stuff in little bottles along one wall too. I figured them to be like paint thinner and such. And lumber. Well, not lumber like you is going to build a house. There was wood slats that looked like what you'd makes frames out of if you didn't already have frames that was already made up whole."

"No artwork though?"

"No, just the stuff to make it from what I seen," Duncan clarified. "What are you getting at?"

"Too long to explain now. We have to go. I'll tell you on the way."

"You seemed to know your way around so far," he said. "But just so we ain't carrying all our eggs in one basket, Ness, call in and have backup meet me and the art expert here at the trailer we was at yesterday. Then you take one of the boys out back and check all the surrounding area. And have the other do a good sweep of the building."

Ness touched his forehead as if in a salute and headed for hallway to the back door.

I turned to my driver, "And you get back to the office and tell them we think we've located Junior Van R." Then to Amiee, "And Amiee, you're coming with us."

"Hold on there!" Duncan interjected. (At least he didn't squelch.) "You might be the expert when it comes to art but I'm the one they gonna hang on a wall if someone gets hurt on this assignment." I'm pretty sure Detective Ness would have pointed to the back of his head if he had still been there to hear that. Duncan continued, "I don't want to go into no showdown dragging no civilian with me. She stays here!"

"I'll take responsibility. Plus, do you want to deal with a hysterical Lily when we get her free?"

"You're pretty optimistic. Okay she can come, but stay in front of her, got it."

"Absolutely," I said. "That's her best side."

WE GOT INTO SGT. DUNCAN'S unmarked, the same car I was in about twelve hours ago that now seemed like a lifetime ago. Duncan took the wheel and Amiee and I piled into the back seat.

From the driver's seat, Duncan half turned toward us and asked, "Okay, so give me the lowdown on why we're heading to where he has to figure we'd go to so it makes it like that's the last place where he should want to be."

"Yeah, Marc," Amiee chimed in, "What he said. I'm wondering about that too. Why are you so sure Junior is going to his trailer?"

I was running on adrenaline now and for the first time I felt on familiar ground and not just half guessing my way around. "When a forger is counterfeiting a work of art, he's doing more than just copying the painting well enough to fool a viewer. He has to reproduce the full experience to get it past the experts. That means the canvas must be right for the period, the paints must be what the original artist would have used. Even the wood has be right."

I held my breath. Amiee was thrown against me as Duncan sped around a corner with tires squealing. "You can't try to pass off a painting that was supposed to be made in the 1800s with an off the shelf stretched canvas from the local art supply shop," I went on, straightening myself up in my seat as Amiee did to herself in hers, "or even with a handmade stretcher built from wood you picked up at Home Depot. You see, it's not just the painting. Copying a picture is easy. Even I can copy a 120-year masterpiece. But forging it. That's something different. The hard part of forging art is making a painting look like it was painted over a century ago while doing it using material from today."

I saw heads nodding in understanding. At least I think it was in understanding and not just because we bounced our way through that last intersection.

Amiee spoke up. "And all that stuff the sergeant found in the trailer is for the, what would you call it, the aging process?"

I continued, "Exactly. Remember all those bottles? Those bottles weren't full of just solvents. They were the chemicals he adds to paint to mimic the composition of what the impressionists were using in the nineteenth century. He certainly has others he uses to age the canvases so they look as old under the paint as the paint does on top of them. And Sarge," I shouted now to be heard over the roaring of the engine as we climbed a big hill, "the wood you found was likely old wood he might have found framing any old art at a thrift shop. He could use it as is, but most likely he takes it apart and he uses the wood to construct his own stretchers. Then to make sure, he'd wash it with something to leave a residue so it looks not just old, but like it's been hanging on a wall collecting dust for a hundred years."

"So he got a lot of stuff there," Duncan cut in. "That still ain't telling me why he risks going back to where we know he might be?"

"Because," I explained as we free fell down the other side of the hill, "we can forensically match that stuff to the paintings we suspect are his work. Those are like his paintings' fingerprints. If we find them, we have proof of his guilt. That's probably why he works out of a trailer. He can keep moving around so we can't get a bead on him. He's going there to protect his investment."

"Or else," Amiee countered, "he's going to destroy the evidence."

"One way or another he's going to that trailer," I said as confidently as I could.

Duncan said, "Well it's as good a theory as I can come up with. We'll see soon enough. It's just another block up and around the corner."

Amiee looked over at me and asked, "When you asked the sergeant what he found at the trailer, why did you make it sound like you knew there wasn't any art."

Another good question but one I had an answer for. "Because he wouldn't risk storing completed pieces and the solvents he used to treat them in the same place. He'd want them separated as soon as possible. And even with all the manipulation of the paint and canvas and wood, he'd still have to let them cure for several weeks, maybe months before he could move them. That means he needs another space for them to hang for that amount of time. I think I know where they are, but I know I know they wouldn't be in the trailer. Unless he was working on one. But I don't think he ever planned to sell his forgeries. He's been selling the originals."

Amiee and Sgt. Duncan both looked confused, but it was Amiee who asked. "You lost me. Where was he getting originals? He's a counterfeiter not a thief."

"That's the third person we're going to find there. Probably. The art thief part of the team. Not a cat burglar type thief but one could swap a specific copy for a specific original."

"Hold onto that part," Duncan eased the car into a drive leading to a strip of about a dozen house trailers parked in a row.

At the end of the row, a large pickup was pulling the last trailer out of its spot. Duncan shouted at us, "Hold on!" He switched on his siren, punched the accelerator and the unmarked leaped halfway down the drive!

Before it even registered on me what we were looking at, the oversized pickup truck pulling a 28-foot office type trailer hurdled toward us then flashed past.

Duncan spun the wheel and set off behind them. He reached for the microphone. "Dispatch, unit 7 in pursuit of a red 250 series pickup pulling a white and red construction trailer registered to Greg Berger of—"

While he continued his transmission, I pulled Amiee closer to me. "I'm sorry I got you into this. You should have stayed at the Hensley."

"I'm okay," Amiee said. "And I'll be okay as long as you're with me. Besides you need me. We're going to catch them, and when we do, I'll be able to help with Lily."

I held her closer.

"Where is that backup Ness ordered?" Duncan asked no one in particular. "Are you guys okay back there?" He asked us as we bounced over a railroad crossing.

"We're good," I shouted over the roar of the unmarked's big block of an engine. "Don't let him ditch that trailer."

"Don't let him hurt Lily!" Amiee added.

The radio crackled, "Unit 7, Unit 5. We're coming south on 47th and see him ahead of us, now turning onto Eighth."

"Five, this is seven. I'm going to swing around and try to get ahead of them," Duncan spoke back to the microphone.

We took a hard right, throwing Amiee as far across the seat as her lap and shoulder belt allowed and pushing my head and shoulder against the window glass. We sped forward two more blocks then pushing us back again we swung left for another block and made yet another hard left on Eighth Avenue. And there they were!

Duncan navigated the big sedan sideways blocking all lanes, skidded to a stop in front of the truck, blocking its path. He jumped out of his seat into a crouch behind the door with his service revolver unholstered and aimed at the front of the truck. "Hands out the window an' come out of the vehicle now!"

Slowly from the passenger side out stepped Gregory Louis Van Rysselberghe, II, aka Junior Van R, aka Greg Berger. Struggling in the back seat I could see a bound and gagged Lily Vance. And sliding off the driver's seat was the seldom seen, fuming mad night maid.

CHAPTER 14~ The Lady Left

The darkness of the night intensified with the storm.
Thunder cracked! Lightning flared! A shot rang out!
A piercing scream filled the air!
Large ships filled the small harbor.
The cannons' roar broke the morning calm!
The sides battled on.
Soon all was quiet even as the action continued
The sun sank below the waves.
Somewhere a dog howled at the moon.
The sun rose abruptly!
Snow fell across the land.
They danced madly in the garden.
A horse bucked while pulling the wagon.
The lady with the parasol walked away.

IT WAS TWO DAYS LATER, and we were sitting in the Hensley's lounge again. Amiee, Lily, Grayson, the Widow Hensley, and myself. Lily was telling us how the maid had been waiting for her when she came out of the shower.

"That was the second shower in as many days that didn't end well. She must have been beside the door because when I came out of the bathroom, she conked me over the head with something." Lily rubbed the back of her head and winced in memory. "I don't remember seeing Junior there but when I came to, he had me over his shoulder like a sack of potatoes, and we were going into that linen closet."

Amiee interrupted Lily's story. "I don't understand how Junior got there. Marc, you were chasing him around the building while we were chasing him down the upstairs hallway."

"Except Berger, err Junior didn't go around the building," I explained. "After he let himself into the ballroom, he let himself into the kitchen through the ballroom wall. Then he went up the service stairs and came out in the upstairs hall just in time to help the maid with Lily."

Lily picked up her story. "While Junior still had me over his shoulder, I came to and started screaming. Then he dropped me on the floor and pushed the door shut but Elwood was already coming through it. The maid conked him on the head, and then they tried to push me down the stairs. I grabbed the rail and held on for all I could. I wasn't going to go anywhere. I kept screaming and then she hit me on the head again. This time I went out for I don't know how long, but when I came to, I was in the back of that pickup and tied up like some poor animal in a rodeo with a gag stuffed in my mouth and tied at the back of my head. We were on some wild ride like a rodeo too. I was certain I was done for and then we screeched to a stop, I fell forward off the seat, and I heard Sgt. Duncan hollering about coming out of the truck."

"Speak of the dirt devil." I pointed to the lounge door where the sergeant himself was walking in on those same old scuffed service boots.

He kept walking right to our table. He singled out Amiee. "If you're here, who's going to get my Yoo-Hoo?"

"No Yoo-Hoo," Amiee sighed. "How about a ginger ale?"

"How about a beer. This here is a social call an' a beer makes me social."

Amiee got up to fetch Sgt. Duncan his brew while he settled into the last chair around the table. "Can I get everyone else a refill?" She asked. All around hands raised and heads nodded in assent.

"Did you ever get anything out of the maid?" I asked Duncan. "Berger couldn't stop talking once we explained we could make the felony murder disappear if he cooperated. He figured a few years in a French prison held a better outlook for his long-term health than a few years on death row here."

"Wait. What?" Lily looked up with a look of shock on her face.

Duncan chuckled. "Oh for sure! For two days she didn't say nothing but that she wants a lawyer. Then she hears through the grapevine that her playmate got a bad case of loose lips. That's when she opened up an' started blamin' everyone but herself." He took a mug of foamy, amber ale from Amiee. "Thank you, missy. You ain't so bad. No wonder our art expert likes you. An' then—"

"Wait!" Lily bounced in her seat trying to interrupt again.

I chuckled, "That's right dear. I love you for your beer."

"Hmm. "Amiee giggled. "A couple days ago it was for my coffee. Art experts can be so fickle," and distributed the rest of the glasses around the table.

"Stop that!" Lily squelched. "Now wait, wait, wait!" She was fully out of her chair now. "What do you mean, make the murder go away? You're going to let him get away with killing my Louie?"

"Berger, or Junior to use the familiar, didn't kill him," Duncan said calmly through the foam he was rubbing off his lips with the back of his hand.

"But that's what Amiee told me. She said Marc figured out how it was all done.

"Yeah," I started to explain. "I had figured out how it was done. But the who I had figured on I figured wrong."

"Then if Junior didn't do it, who did? I don't suppose the butler did it." Lily asked

"The butler never does it," Amiee tossed in. "Don't you ever read mysteries."

"The maid did it?" Lily wondered aloud.

"Nope, not her either." Duncan supplied while holding his glass halfway to his mouth.

"Who else is there?" Lily asked with an extra puzzled expression.

"C'mon Sarge," Amiee looked around at the variety of glasses around the table, all seemingly suspended in midair. "you're being cruel and unusual. Lily has a right to know. And I want to know, too."

"Okay," Duncan set his glass down. "I shouldn't tell you this because I ain't on duty, but...oh what the hell. It was only one sip of beer." He reached to the leather pouch attached to his belt and pulled out his handcuffs. "C'mon there, Mr. Grayson. You know the drill. You should. You've been through it enough times."

"It *was* the butler," Lily, Amiee, and the Widow said in unison.

"Hands behind your back." Duncan snapped the cuffs around Grayson's wrists. "You're under arrest for the murder of G. Louis Vance, the Third." Then into his lapel he said, "Okay, you can come get him."

After everybody closed their mouths and blinked a few times, Amiee started with the obvious question. "Grayson! Who knew?"

"Apparently G. Louis knew," I answered and filled them in on some of the intel Berger, alias Junior Van R had given us. "Grayson, real name Guillermo Rosales, we think real name Guillermo Rosales, was the mastermind behind the thefts and forgeries."

Detective Ness and a pair of uniformed officers walked in. The uniforms took custody of Grayson. Ness came over to the table. "Hi Lily, err, Mrs. Vance." Then to Duncan "Who gets him first?"

"We do," Duncan answered. "Murder trumps theft and forgery. If the insurance company wants to prosecute, they got a couple ways to do to. Crossley will handle that end."

"Bye Woody," Lily waved to Ness, all eyes now turned toward her.

After a moment to digest that, Duncan said to me, "You wanna keep going."

I picked up the narrative. "Yeah." I cleared my throat. "Rosales, if that is his real name, met Berger in France a lifetime ago. Like his antecedent, Berger was a decent artist but a better copier. He also was a genius at aging art and was making a brisk business doing forgeries and passing them off as the real thing. Except it was a slow process for one man. Enter Rosales. He took charge of finding and grooming the marks, finding out their favorite artists, and suddenly coming across a formerly unknown original, wouldn't you know.

"It was going well when Berger had the accident in the studio that maimed Louis III. He wanted out. He shuffled little Louie to a convent then he and Rosales packed up and moved here. Rosales, who had previously targeted but never connected with old man Hensley, remembered he was some kind of fanatic collector of impressionist art. He presented himself to Mr. Hensley as a gentleman's gentleman and secured a position here. He likely thought he found his own paradise to settle in as a retirement home surrounded day and night by priceless masterpieces. I'm sure, in the back of his mind he also thought he found a new spot to launch into a retirement job moving those priceless masterpieces."

I stopped long enough to whet my whistle then continued. "Rosales changed his name, weaseled his way in here as the old man's man servant back when here was just the Hensley manor, and not The Hensley Manor, and all was good. Until it wasn't. After a while he realized Hensley wasn't just a collector but a collector extraordinaire. And that whet his whistle. But it was too risky for him to try anything. When the old man decided to turn this place into an inn, his wheels started turning. He figured with it opened to the public, they'd be a new chance of diverting blame with every new vacationer. He looked up Junior and talked him into cleaning his brushes and picking up where he left off in the old country. Rosales, now Grayson, recommended van Rysselberghe, now Berger, for the handyman position, sweet talked an old flame to be the night maid to do the actual swap, and the business was up and running again."

I stopped long enough to take another sip of my bourbon and water and saw that everyone else was still on the edges of their seats.

I continued, "Shortly after that we started hearing about originals we knew should be here showing up on walls where they didn't belong.

"According to Junior, he panicked when Lily and Lou checked in. Rosales/Grayson knew about Lou's skin condition and remembering what happened to Louie Three, figured it couldn't be a coincidence.

"Berger/Junior said he wanted to talk to his son. Grayson/Rosales wouldn't have it. He was afraid the family ties were still there, and he didn't want them in the same room. During the interrogation, Berger said Rosales went to Lou to try to buy him off. When he didn't go for that, Rosales waited a couple days, then took him out with the eucalyptus oil in the water glass. He had the maid do the actual work of planting the oil and wrapping the canvas around Lou's neck to frame me. All that was Rosales' idea."

"Poor Lou. He probably didn't notice the oil in his water because he always smelled it on himself. It wasn't too bad to be honest about it," Lily reminisced. "You're probably wondering and you're all so sweet not to ask, but Louie never knew Junior was his father. Or at least never told me if he suspected it. We both were doing research on Glafira Rosales and then found what looked like her scam was active again. It led us here because of the art involved, not the people. Marc, is Grayson, or Rosales, related to Glafira?"

"We haven't found a connection yet." I answered. "We're not even sure Rosales is his real name, but he certainly idolized Glafira Rosales. He has all sorts of articles and writings about her up in his room."

I went on to explain that Glafira Rosales was a scam artist who flooded the market with fake mid-century abstracts bringing down the famous Knoedler Gallery in the process. "What she did with phony

Pollocks, he wanted to do with fake Monets. He heard about the Hensley collection and wormed his way in here. He knew where all the pieces were, even the ones not displayed. Like Glafira, he wasn't an artist and had to find someone to create the pieces. Enter Junior Van R. his buddy from across the sea. The maid came on board so she could access the rooms and move the art around. Remember in the car when I said Berger needed somewhere to hang his copies to cure? That somewhere was here, and the maid was instrumental in hiding Junior's pieces in storage areas and then moving them in place when they were ready to be displayed, swapping them for originals."

I needed a big gulp after all that. "And there we have the whole gang all in one tidy location."

"I can't take any more of this!" The Widow Hensley, wearing a green business skirt suit with off-white pumps and an emerald head band, rose to her feet. "I just wanted an easy ride in life, and I found it. I even liked that old guy and then his heart exploded. Now I'm stuck with this place. Forged art, gun toting guests, exploding elevators, killer employees! I've had it! Tomorrow the place goes up for sale."

"I'll buy it right now," Lily said and stood up at her place across the table from the Widow. "I know, Louie was killed here but I like it here, and Amiee knows how to make a Boulevardier like nobody else. I think Louie would want to settle here. Maybe his ghost already is here so his money might as well be stuck here too."

The Widows eyes widened. "You mean really? You can afford it then?"

"No problem. Louie made a fortune in essential oils futures. Let's go sign some papers. Amiee, you chill us a bottle of champagne and we'll all have a party."

EPILOGUE

The darkness of the night intensified with the storm.
Thunder cracked! Lightning flared! A shot rang out!
A piercing scream filled the air!
Large ships filled the small harbor.
The cannons' roar broke the morning calm!
The sides battled on.
Soon all was quiet even as the action continued
The sun sank below the waves.
Somewhere a dog howled at the moon.
The sun rose abruptly!
Snow fell across the land.
They danced madly in the garden.
A horse bucked while pulling the wagon.
The lady with the parasol walked away.
And they lived happily ever after!

"THIS IS GREAT! WHEN you told me to make sure I had my passport I thought we were going to Paris. I never imagined Norway." Amiee was unpacking, "I brought a bathing suit but there probably won't be a lot of sunbathing on this trip."

This trip was a month-long cruise on the good ship Aurora, sailing out of Anchorage through the Arctic Ocean to Oslo.

It was a month later and indictments had been handed down for Junior/Berger for forgery, theft, and conspiracy, for the maid for murder and theft, and all the above plus conspiracy to commit murder for Grayson/Rosales. After we had inventoried all the paintings including those in storage, we discovered over half of the collection had been swapped for counterfeit and hustled off to underground art auctions. Rosales had kept impeccable records, and we were able to recover nearly all the originals. The company was so grateful for breaking up such a notorious ring, they gave me a month off and a bonus big enough to buy two vacations of a lifetime. Or one vacation for two lives.

"I think when Lily found out where I was going, she would have given me three months off." Amiee exclaimed. "Even she hasn't been over the top of the world and she's been everywhere."

"It will be a first for me too, Amiee," I said. "I'm not sure what I'm looking forward to more – a month with you or a month away from chasing bad guys."

"Well you better decide soon because one way or another I'm warming up a deck chair," then looking at the snow flurries drifting past the cabin's little window, "or maybe a bar stool for the next thirty days."

"Oh Amiee, you know I'd take thirty days with you even if I had to work all thirty of them." I stowed the last of the luggage under the bed. "Let's go on deck and watch Alaska get smaller."

Just then there was a knock at the door. I opened it to a purser's assistant holding a small envelope. "Message for Mr. Crossley."

"Thank you," I said as I took the envelope and opened it. I frowned. "Amiee? How would you feel about 30 days with me if I was working?"

"Thirty days with you doing anything is still a dream come true." She stopped folding and looked at me. "Wait! What? Mister Agent Marc Crossley, what are you hinting at?"

"Well, um, maybe they just want to wish us a bon voyage, but I have to call the office when we reach Nome."

"Arrggghh!"

And that's when I found out cruise ship pillows hurt when hurled across the very small space of a ship's cabin.

~TO BE CONTINUED~

Bonus~ Meet Marc

Hi. Hello. Pleased to meet you. My name is Marc, Marc Crossley. First off, I want to thank you for reading our first adventure, *Bad Impressions*. I came up with that title. Really. I said it in what I think it was Chapter 4, but somewhere in the editing process it ended up on the cutting room floor or wherever the things you don't want in a book go. I'm not so sure about that because this is the first time I've ever appeared in a book, or booklet, or whatever this ends up being. Actually, I'm more of a movie person.

And that's why you're here. To find out more about me. You really didn't get a lot of my story other than I am an insurance investigator specializing in art. You don't even know the name of the company. That would be Triplett Brothers Assurance Agents and Underwriters. Don't let the name fool you. It's not a set of triplets who own the firm. It's not even a single Triplett. There hasn't been a Triplett in the company for the last hundred years, and it's been around a lot longer than that. Stories have it that the firm was founded in London sometime in the fifteenth century, by four brothers and a cousin. I guess the cousin was a pseudo-sibling. By the time I came on board, there wasn't a Triplett in sight.

I joined the Triplett firm, oh gee, it must have been about 12 years ago. I had always been interested in art, and I think I'm not a bad artist myself. I didn't kid myself though. I couldn't then and can't now imagine making any kind of a living as an artist. Oh sure, there are people who work on ad campaigns, or as graphic artists or animators, and there is always teaching, but none of them let you express yourself like Warhol. Do you know who makes the real money in the art world? Forgers.

I remember seeing a documentary about forged artwork and their forgers quite some time ago. Not as far back as when the Tripletts were putting together their company. I think it was in the seventies. Um, the 1970s that is. *F is for Fake* written by Orson Welles was the documentary in question. I think it was a documentary, but maybe with a little extra. If you know Welles' works, then you know he doesn't constrain himself to a single genre at a time.

Anyway, the docuwhatever explored the 'career' of (suspected) notorious art forger Elmyr de Hory. It opened my eyes to how many paintings hanging in public may well not be what they are purported to be. Or to have been done by those other than who they are purported to be done by. (Don't worry, I'll ask the editor to fix the grammar in that before this goes to print.)

It was after that realization that I decided if the real money in art (outside those few masterpieces that make the artists oodles of dollars but not until well after their death) goes to the forgers of the world, then the second biggest pot should be raked in by those who catch them. I was quite wrong about that, but I decided to join the small group of people dedicated to seeing that only the real masters are hung on walls around the world anyway. I didn't realize that until I was just a few weeks away from graduating with my BFA and immediately withdrew my acceptance to a Master of Fine Arts program and began to explore criminal justice programs.

It may not be the most financially rewarding career, but it is intellectually and emotionally rewarding. And educationally rewarding. As I said in the Prologue, Triplett is a specialty insurer of works of art, sculptures, precious gems, and the types of doodads that the rich and famous tend to collect and insure. As such, I've gotten to extend my knowledge base to include sculptures, precious gems, and fancy doodads, and expand my circle to experts in those other fields and the folk who are lucky enough (and wealthy enough) to collect said arts and works.

I've been lucky also to meet some other fantastic people as I've plied my trade and investigated disappearances and over-appearances of some of the world's most beautiful baubles. Like Amiee. (She's one of the fantastic people, not a beautiful bauble, although she is as beautiful as anything Monet ever put to canvas.)

I am convinced Amiee and I are destined to find ourselves in the middle of more adventures like the one we walked into at the Hensley. (Well, I walked into it. She was already there at the Hensley even if she wasn't already there in the adventure.) There are a lot of baubles to get lost in the world and a lot of investigating to do in the search for them. In the Epilogue you already got a hint that we might be on a new adventure sooner than we thought we would be. I can't think of anybody I'd rather share my time investigating with than that dark haired, blue-eyed beauty. In fact, I can't think of anybody I'd rather investigate than that dark haired, blue-eyed beauty, but that's an entirely different story. (And she really can make a Boulevardier like nobody else.)

Look for us in more Adventures of Marc and Amiee. And look for a few other special people you might remember from the case of the *Bad Impressions*.

Oh, in case you are wondering, the Triplett firm, at least as far as I've described it here, doesn't really exist. Neither does Hensley Manor. And then quite technically, neither do I. Now, Orson Welles does exist and so does or did Elmyr de Hory, and Welles really did feature Elmyr in the 1973 documentary *F is for Fake*. (The guy working the keyboard said I should make all that clear.)

Warhol exists also – or rather existed. (The keyboard guy didn't say anything about my having to clarify that, but I thought since I mentioned him, I should put that in there. I may be a figment of someone's imagination, but Andy Warhol isn't, and I don't want anyone misconstruing anything because I didn't clarify it.) The impressionists might have been all over *Bad Impressions*, but Warhol is my personal favorite. Maybe he can be in a future adventure. (Hey writer guy! What do you think?)

Well, that's me. I'll see you in the next adventure!

Bonus~ Meet Amiee

Hello! I'm Amiee, Boulevardier maker extraordinaire. Let me say right from the top, if you've not had a Boulevardier, you are keeping yourself from experiencing a little piece of Heaven. It was created in the 1920s by American socialite Erskine Gwynne, while living in Paris. You may know him as the writer who founded a literary magazine *The Boulevardier*. (That's true. The who, the what, and the where. Really!) A Boulevardier is whiskey, Campari, and sweet vermouth. You can look up the proportions, but my recipe is my secret. It's no secret though that I use bourbon for the whiskey component. Some other mixologists use rye. That works well too though just a tad too sweet for me.

So, now that we have that out of the way (I knew you were wondering about it), let me tell you a little something about myself. So far as you know I might not have existed until I showed up as the bartender at the Hensley Manor. To be honest, that's when the most interesting part of my life began.

Before I got to the Hensley, I didn't really do much of anything of consequence. After high school I went to college, but I never clicked with any program. I took a few general courses, and I loved the learning part, but I can't say that I saw any sort of future for me after school and eventually I figured I could keep on learning just by going to the library every week.

While I was looking for ways to finance my 'education,' I discovered bartending. Or the lowest common denominator of keeping a bar, and keeping those who visit it happy. I was pouring shots and pulling beers at your basic neighborhood dive bar. The thing about blue collar bars like that, people tip like it's their last day on earth and the last thing they need to do before heading to wherever their promised land might be is to empty their wallets.

I was living on my wages and saving my tips to open my own dive bar except I wanted a classy dive bar. May even a bar and grill. To that end, I went to the local community college for hospitality management. One of my classmates was another dreamer looking for her way into the restaurant business. That was Eileen. You didn't meet her. She found out Old Man Hensley was converting his manse into a 'country inn' and jumped on the opportunity. She was still working at the Hensley when the case of the *Bad Impressions* went down but was on vacation, so she missed all the excitement. Now that I think about it, she had some excitement of her own. She came back with a rock on her ring finger that would have made the Hope Diamond jealous and stayed just long enough to give her couple weeks' notice.

But you don't want to know about her, you want to know about me! Besides being adorable, Marc makes it sound like I'm some exotic woman because I have dark hair and blue eyes. My whole family is a bunch of blue-eyed brunettes. They say it's common enough among the Irish, Spanish, and southern Italians. I think I have some of all of that in some or another branch of my family tree. It works for me. Blue is my favorite color, but you probably figured that out because of how I keep the ends of my hair dyed blue. I do that because my father is a prostate cancer survivor, and because it's the color of sapphire, my birthstone. And I think it caught Marc's eye, so there was that too.

Oh, right, I started telling you about Eileen and how she heard about how the Hensley manor was becoming The Hensley Manor. She got the job as kitchen and banquet manager and ask me to be in charge of the bar there. Sorry, the lounge. It wasn't my own place, and it wasn't the tip haven the dive bar was, but it suited me. The hours were good and how often do you get to work surrounded by some of the world's greatest works of art without working in a museum?

While I was there, I met some really interesting people. Even before Marc showed up. There seems to be a special sort of person who visits a place like the Hensley. It's not a regular hotel, not even a B&B. Now that I think about it, there's no place else like the Hensley. Oh, I said "while I was there," but that's not accurate. I still am there. I don't know if I'll ever leave it, except for another adventure like the case of the *Bad Impressions*. It was a fun few days, if you can call murder fun. And don't forget the explosion and 'fire.'

Still, I got to meet Marc. I know we'll have more good times and adventures coming our way. And I got to meet Lily (with one 'L', or two but not two in a row, depending on how you want to look at it). I was a little leery of her when she and Lou first checked in, but I found out she's a great person and she has become a terrific friend. I see myself seeing more of her in the future too.

So that's a little more about me. I'm sure that when you follow me and Marc (what? oh okay) Marc and I... (Wait. No, I don't care if you're the one working the keyboard. Marc and I isn't right in this case.) (Dumb authors.) I'm sure that when you follow me and Marc (okay, Marc and me (sheesh)) in our future adventures, you will find out even more about me. Personally, I can't wait for the next one, *Ice Breaker*. We get to sail over the top of the world! Can you believe it?

I will look for you then, with some surprises only Marc would be able to come up with. With my help of course. See you aboard!

Note from the Author

All the works of art mentioned in this novel are real and to the best of my knowledge are correctly attributed to artist and date of first exhibition. Any errors are mine alone. Also, to the best of my knowledge, none are currently displayed in any quaint country inn.

The historical figures also are real. To a point. All of the artists mentioned, including Théophile "Theo" van Rysselberghe, were real people. Theo's extended family as depicted in this novel is a figment of my imagination.

Glafira Rosales (aka Glafira Gonzalez, aka Glafira Rosales Rojas) is quite real and in 2013 admitted to moving more than 60 "lost" works by abstract expressionists like Jackson Pollock, Mark Rothko, Robert Motherwell and Willem de Kooning through the Manhattan based Knoedler Art Gallery from 1994 to 2011. As a non-artist, she solicited the services of art forger Pei-Shen Qian to copy the paintings she in turn sold as originals. The Knoedler, founded in 1846, closed in 2011 for "business reasons." Our Guillermo Rosales and his gang are fictional characters. If Ms. Rosales has any relatives or fans known as Guillermo, it is completely coincidental.

At the time of writing this book, the good ship Aurora indeed exists and indeed there have been commercial cruises that sail over the top of the world from Anchorage to Oslo. Whether the Aurora has ever sailed this route with or without our intrepid couple is unknown.

Michael Ross, September 2025

Acknowledgements

Books may bear the author's name on the cover, but it takes many others to turn the words into a story. My heartfelt thanks go to those who took their time and exercised their patience with me including the many I will undoubtedly forget until I click "send" and release this work on the world.

The ones I do remember and include here are Diem P and Susy F for the push to put those first words down when this was intended to be just a lark of a short story, for Angelica R who was the first to read the first draft and had the grace to say it had promise, to Mary Ann W who was the first to read the second draft and had the grace to say it was promising, to Patti R and Mary Anne R who edited the third draft when I felt the promise was strong enough to withstand more rigorous scrutiny, and to my wonderful team of readers who validated the almost final final draft.

Other nameless wonders are all the art teachers I've had who didn't know it then but gave me something I used in life that was more useful than what all the calculus teachers gave me, and all those who contributed to the many and varied post, articles, and snippets found on the internet.

Finally, a special thanks to author and screenwriter Rick Ley who took time from his own projects to explain the process of creating a book from thoughts in the mind to a book on a shelf. A better mentor and friend I could not ask for.

About the Author

After a full and successful career in the health professions Michael searched for something to do. Always at his best when he was behind a keyboard writing those dull medical articles, he took to writing more upbeat, energetic, and fun pieces.

Since retiring from the heath care scene, Michael has written over 200 blog articles for the 'Uplift!' inspirational blog found on ROAMcare.org. A reasonable amateur artist and a voracious reader, he naturally wondered if he could not duplicate the success he's had with short motivational articles in the fiction world, specifically mysteries, specifically mysteries that add a little artistic flair to the story.

"I like nothing better than to spend a quiet evening with a good mystery. The more murders, the better," he'd often joke.

Bad Impressions is the first fiction he's published but not the only one he's written. He expects books two and three following more exploits of Marc and Amiee to be released shortly.

Michael lives alone but within walking distance of his only daughter right outside Pittsburgh, Pennsylvania and has a penchant for fries on his salad and in his sandwiches.

Coming Attractions

Ice Breaker - Available early 2026

Marc and Amiee are setting off on the adventure or a lifetime, a monthlong cruise over the North Pole. But first Marc has to finish the paperwork from his most recent case, a missing Japanese netsuke, not very valuable but a treasured keepsake.

Now that case is done, and their bags are packed, they can set on their adventure. But is it and can they?

Join our favorite couple as they play hide and seek with a killer at sea.

THE GOLDEN HOUR - COMING Spring 2026

Marc and Amiee are finding time to be alone more precious that gold. And more elusive too. Where will Marc and Amiee's third adventure take them?

THE AUTHORPRENEUR NEWSLETTER

Writing is a business. That's why Michael calls his newsletter "The Authorpreneur." Subscribe at the website and always know where Marc and Amiee can be found, other projects Michael has on tap, what he's reading, a look inside the business of writing and self-publishing, and whatever next up might be.

Subscribe at www.michaelrossmedia.com[1] to stay up to date with Michael, Maarc and Amiee, and the rest of those hanging out at the Hensley

---

1.   http://www.michaelrossmedia.com